ARDENT PASSION

VS

THE TREE OF LIVING WATER

RANDY YOUNG

Printed in the United States of America
First Printing 2020
First Edition 2020

ISBN: 978-1-7330041-6-9

10 9 8 7 6 5 4 3 2 1

Published & Distributed by:
Iqra Publishing Inc.
157 Sunset Avenue
Atlanta, GA 30314
www.iqrapublishing.com

Edited by: Chief Editor: Lori McCaskil, Developmental Editor: Terry
Askew
Structure/Line Editor: Angelica Polis

Chapter 1

---

1 Chronicles 16:11

Ajayi sprinted onto the back porch at "Christ in All", a small Christian church in the Phillips neighborhood. The turf belonged to his rivals: The 13th Street boys, an offshoot of the notorious Blood street gang. The young banger ducked behind a large stainless-steel gas grill. He sat motionless doing his best to control his breathing because not doing so might alert his pursuers to his exact position. The two thugs were right on his heels and if Ajayi hadn't jumped over that privacy fence half a block away, they would have shot him in the back.

"O' girl messed the whole jack move!" He thought to himself. Tristan, Ajayi's childhood friend, was robbed by two other members from the 13th St. boys just last week. He was

1

standing outside JJ's Soul Food on Carlson Blvd., one block east of Norfolk High where they attended. Tristan was jacked for his new Retro 4's and his iPhone 11. He was also shot in the abdomen, rendering him in critical condition requiring medical attention on the sixth floor inside General Hospital in downtown Norfolk.

Ajayi was on some get back until a little girl riding her Big Wheel rolled right into the line of fire. As Ajayi held the strap to Shannon's head, the barrel was pointed right at his rival and the bullet would have rippled into his forehead between the teenager's eyes. Shots rang out and sprinklers sprayed in Ajayi's hair, face and clothes as the gang bangers caught up to him. Bullets ricocheted off the windowsill flying over his head. Ajayi raised the strap above his head pulling the trigger. Nothing happened, only a click and then another click. He squeezed harder but the clip was empty as a result of firing all seventeen bullets during his escape from a jack move gone bad.

"Thirteenth baby!" one of his pursuers yelled.

Several more shots rang out, then the loud chirp from an east end Norfolk police cruiser. Speeding up the alley sent his rivals running east in the direction of Moreland Ave. "Oh, snap!" Ajayi heard one of them say. The loud sound from the siren overpowered every other police cruiser with audible noise. A couple of minutes went by before he peeked around the gas grill, listening for any movements. Ajayi took the chance to reposition himself because his weight was mostly on his left ankle, causing it to ache. Nothing was heard in the vicinity, no one seen in the area except the siren of the cruiser allowing him to know its location at that precise moment. This prompted him to look over his shoulder in the direction of the window where there was a low murmuring coming from the other side of the wood siding wall.

Ajayi looked around checking out the small enclosed porch space. The cloudy day cast tainted lighting on the porch. Other than the grill, there was a bright red ten-speed bicycle laying on its side. The galvanized steel handlebar had white handle grips with red, white and blue plastic ribbons protruding from the ends. The bike also had a one-foot square wire basket mounted over the front tire. Beside the bike was a mud filled dark traffic worn green welcome mat. Ajayi was stooping on the left side of the back door next to a stack of four black plastic milk crates filled with old newspapers, soda cans and plastic drink bottles.

Again, he peeked up over the wood-sided wall for his pursuers, checking to see if indeed the coast was clear. He saw the police cruiser at the end of the alley now with its emergency lights flashing. With the siren now silent, Ajayi saw Shannon and his homeboys bent over the hood of the cruiser with their hands interlocked on top of their heads. Ajayi turned and slid back down into a sitting position. He looked at the Glock Z3 in his hand thinking, "I can't step back out there like this." But walking through this neighborhood without his strap would be close to signing a death warrant having no insurance policy. And that was considered slipping if you asked his homies.

However, with the police everywhere, he would have to walk his rivals' blocks naked and uninsured until he reached the train station three blocks away. Ajayi searched for a spot to hide his heat. After things cooled down a bit, he would backtrack to retrieve his insurance policy. Still brainstorming, he had an 'aha' moment, "Aha, the crates!" he thought. He stooped low, carefully easing back to the milk crates, trying not to attract attention to himself. Reaching the crates, he lifted the first one and placed it on the wooden deck floor followed by the other two to reach the crate at the bottom. This crate had many empty water bottles filled to the brim.

Ajayi thrusted his hand amidst the bottles making his way down to the bottom while pushing the bottles to the side and placed the Glock in the crate. He then let the bottles fall back in place to cover the weapon. He restacked the crates, stood and dusted off his dark blue khakis. That's when he noticed the small hole in his coat under his right armpit. A bullet had ripped a hole in his three-quarter length leather London Fog coat, but he hadn't been shot, and that was a good thing. He looked up at the sound of winter ice crushing under the tires of an unmarked black police SUV heading towards Moreland Ave, where the other cruisers were. The black Tahoe swayed from side to side as it rolled over the uneven ice patches in the alley.

Ajayi leaned up against a porch support post in a manner that said he belonged on that back porch. And having just tucked the strap, he was confident in eyeing down the police's SUV. Through all the commotion on the outside of the building, Ajayi noticed that the murmuring never changed or stopped coming from inside the church.

Being from Norfolk, Virginia, he only knew one type of lifestyle, survival of the fittest.

Ajayi joined the Westside Crips at the age of nine after nearly being stomped to death on his way home from school one day. Since Ajayi didn't have any siblings, it was just him and his mom, Alicia. He needed support and protection from the Bloods on the opposite end of his block. Ajayi felt that joining a crew that felt the same way about his attackers as him made perfect sense. This thought process would get him to hook up with Tristan. The two were put on the same day by being jumped into the set. Ajayi also hung around his uncle Damon, who showed him how to sell work and take care of himself.

From the tender age of nine, he began to sell yayo, gang banged, and robbed to eat. Damon was an OG Crip and would always fill his nephew's ears with his own motto: "Take what you want, 'cause it's a dog-eat-dog world." The bond was tight between him and his uncle. So, when Damon was shot and killed outside a carwash in a jack move gone bad, the murder sparked a violent side in Ajayi that many around the hood had never seen. Afterwards, just the mention of Ajayi's name caused many including his enemies to get their act together.

Chapter 2

Psalm 86:11

T here was a sense of peace as the seventeen-year old banger stood still wondering about the constant murmuring on the other side of the wall. He took a step closer to the back window, peeking in. The room appeared to be a small kitchen, and to his left, catty corner from where he peered in, was a pale green and white sixties style refrigerator with a long metallic handle extended across the front of the door. There was a green table with four metal legs ten feet away from the fridge. Four picnic style chairs were tucked under each side of the table.

The table was close to Ajayi, and he could see a stack of white napkins with strawberry prints on them. To the right was a counter with a leaking sink and a microwave that displayed the time, 3:45 PM. However, it was the short white man kneeling with his hands together that satisfied Ajayi's curiosity. Ajayi could see that the man that he looked upon was praying, so that's where the murmuring was coming from. Salt and pepper hair, in the prostrate position, he just kept repeating, "Thank you God...thank you God..." The man would eventually get up, look around, and see everything transpiring at that hour, even visiting the back porch where Ajayi had stashed his Glock Z3.

The young banger shook his head and whispered, "Fake," under his breath. "If God is real," he thought, "Then how are all of my homeboys dropping?" It was a trying time for Ajayi, people he knew were dying every day. The murder rate was up in Norfolk. Approaching mid-2016, the murder rate was nearly one hundred per month with just under five hundred murders by June. His grandmother, Dolores, would drag him to church where Pastor Coleman, the leader of Grace Temple, spoke of Jesus Christ the anointed savior. When she took him with her to church, he rarely payed attention or got involved in any meaningful or spiritual way. He sat there texting his homeboys, getting updates on his enemies and whatever's cracking around the hood.

Ajayi's uncle, Damon, would also plant a seed of darkness over the seed of light every time. Ajayi returned to the hood from church saying things like, "Church is for scary niggas, and Jesus wasn't white...he was black." It was all very plastic to a confused Ajayi, so he rejected the teachings concerning Christ.

Alicia was asleep late afternoon, twisting and turning as though an evil spirit had her in a nightmarish clutch. Feverishly sweating, she wrestled with her subconscious to awaken from the vivid omen, but the horror pressed on relentlessly.

Virtually appearing was a colossal Romanesque coliseum that rose up from the ground in Central Norfolk. The stadium was filled with a homogenous albino audience, barely covered in shreds of bleach spotted red velvet. They all stood simultaneously as Ajayi entered at meridian through the portal of the east, the eye of the needle.

He was facing a matador outfitted in white and gold with a red cape. Whipping a muleta in his right hand while grasping a crystal sword in his left with a devious grin on his bronzed face. As Ajayi approached, a creepy, massive, fierce albino bull galloped out of nowhere towards the matador, and he taunted it, snapping the red cape and waving it before the bull. The more he whipped and waved the muleta, the bull's eyes changed gradually from pink to a deep red while snorting with fury as dense clouds of steam billowed from its nostrils, rising up to heaven. While digging its right front hoof into the earth then switching to its left, he dug a shallow grave. The motion and rich red color of the muleta magnetized its attention, enraging it, spiking its killer instinct. For some reason, the mutant albino wasn't colorblind, so he was able to see color like humans, unlike any other bull.

Practically drained of blood with varicose veins hyper-exposed, the audience chanted in unison with a loud and demonically portrayed ritualistic, "Ajayi, Ajayi, Ajayi"... "Ajayi, Ajayi, Ajayi." Six times, they uttered his name with a slight pause after the sixth cry then shouted, revealing the name of the bull, "All hail Miura Diablo." Iteratively, they repeated this six-cry chant twice more, each time shouting "All hail Miura Diablo!" Then with a thunderous clap all at once, the white bull chased Ajayi around the arena six times and each time the matador would stab it in the eye until one eye bled profusely of a red crystalline blood.

Then the seventh time around, Veneno, the fastest bull of the underworld burst through the eastern eye of the needle running alongside Miura Diablo causing the bull to gallop with increased stamina and speed. Quickly reaching Ajayi, Miura Diablo lowered its sword like horns, preparing to gore and lift him to oblivion.

But at this very moment, Alicia twisted violently in her sleep toward her nightstand, knocking over a glass of water. Just then, a flood of living water gushed like a river towards Ajayi sweeping him off his feet, saving him from sudden and certain death. A blinding flash of light from the matador's crystal sword as he lifted it to strike Miura Diablo one final time, but he was gored by Veneno, the fastest bull of all time.

With a deep startling inhale, a releasing gasp, Alicia's eyes stretched wide open. She snapped out of the daymare, sitting straight up in the bed gasping for air, frantically grasping for her phone which escaped the stream of water from the overturned glass of water.

Drenched in sweat, an odorous smell of onion and garlic rose from her skin and sheets as she immediately speed dialed her son.

Ajayi's phone rung, causing him to flinch; it was mom. Ajayi stepped off the back porch and out of the warmth of the enclosed space in exchange for a biting 10° wind chill that cut right through him, answering her call.

"Hey mom!" He forced a smile against the arctic wind.

"Hey baby, you alright? Baby, where are you?" she replied seriously on edge.

"Yeah ma, I'm good."

He walked into the alleyway looking up towards Moreland. Ajayi used the phone to also shield his face slightly as he walked up the alley towards the action.

"Ma, why you sound like that? What's going on?"

There's a pathway he planned to take just up on the right about two houses away from the location of the police. The ice was slippery as he approached the path. Avoiding slipping and falling, he thought about Tristan in that same instance.

"Oh, and ma, did you hear anything about Tristan?"

"I had a really bad dream, that's all, but it frightened me. And no, ain't nobody called, not even his mom, Queen. But where are you Ajayi? You ain't safe baby...them streets ain't safe for you."

"On the east side."

"What? Did you just hear me? Now I feel even stronger about you being on the East Side 'cause this dream was too real. It's too dangerous, and I feel like God is tryna tell me somethin', but it ain't making sense right now. It's so horrible, all the senseless murders over there and, this dream. I don't know what it means. I got a bad feeling baby that..."

"Mama!"

"Don't mama me! What are you going over there for?"

"Seeing a friend of mine. Listen ma, I'm on my way home, okay."

"Ajayi, don't lie to me and don't patronize me!"

"Honestly, I'm on my way home ma!" He said before hanging up the phone.

"Ajayi, Ajayi, Ajayi!" She called back but he didn't answer.

Shannon still bent over the hood of the cruiser and locked eyes with Ajayi just before he stepped onto the snowy pathway. There was a small opening ten feet into the path off to the side where an old discarded yellow and green flower pattern love sofa lay flipped on its back. Empty liquor bottles and empty beer cans littered the opening. Halfway through

14

the pathway was a big stone with burnt stains etched into it. Ajayi looked past it all and stepped onto the sidewalk running along Charles Avenue. Cautiously, he strolled towards home three blocks, all 13th territory. He made a mental note of landmarks, stores and street names: All he would use to get back to the church where his strap was. He felt weird all of sudden, something spooked him.

A white 2002 Ford Taurus caked in salt from the roads pulled up beside him as he walked towards home. Ajayi was now only half a block from the train station, where he would board a train that would haul him out of the hostile environment. The windows were tinted, so he didn't know who was behind the wheel, but the way that the car crept beside him indicated that the occupants were a stark contrast to any welcoming committee.

Ajayi slipped his right hand under his coat, playing the role for a moment as though he was packing. Whatever the case, he knew that one false move could trigger a life or death situation. "Just a couple more steps, baby," he thought. Straight ahead was Haron Ave., a major strip in that end of the urban area. It was crime infested. It ran north and south through the east side, up and down as far as the eye could see, lined with small businesses, hair shops, pawn shops, liquor stores, and the major marts, Walmart and K-mart were opposite each other. The North Street train station was across from where Ajayi presently stood on the corner of Charles and Haron Blvd.

His heart was beating fast, as the gray exhaust smoke from the white Taurus floated into the air and up towards heaven while the car revved its engine six times, snorting like a bull drudging the ground before attacking. The phantom seemingly waited for the traffic to clear as if it were party to lurking imminent danger, waiting for the right moment to strike. What would the creepy white Taurus do next? Where would it go? Turn left, right, or go straight across Haron? Six more dramatic seconds seemed like six minutes passed before the white phantom raced into traffic, turning right, south of Haron. Ajayi instantly exhaled, relieved that the threat had all but vanished. Ajayi watched the taillights disappear as the Ford distanced itself. He wondered if the mysterious driver was looking back at him in his rearview mirror thinking, "We will meet again!"

Ajayi needed to get home safely. His mother frantically impressed upon him that his life was in danger, along with the weird experience with the white Taurus, driving him home as quickly as possible.

Ajayi needed to figure a way to safely get back to the church within the next twelve hours or risk someone recycling his weapon with the plastic bottles.

Chapter 3

II Corinthians 1:3-5

One week had passed since the young black kid ran onto the back porch. Pastor Jonathan Briggs was arranging the letters inside the display case outside Christ in All Church near the sidewalk.

Pastor Briggs placed the last letter 'S' in its place. "There!" he said to himself. "A FRAGILE FORGIVENESS," he said out loud to an imaginary congregation. A practice he had adopted for the past ten years. On Wednesdays, he would prepare and get ready for the real thing on Sunday where he'd stand before Christ In All Church members, feeding the flock, preaching out of the bread of life.

It was midday, and the sun was shining through the clouds while the snow fell lightly. He began to think back to that day, a week prior, while on his knees, Pastor Briggs recalls that he saw the young man and had at first thought that he was going to kick the door in. But after seeing the expression on the kid's face, the pastor instantly became an intercessor for him. The look on the young man's face that day was that of a soul needing God. So that's what he prayed for. He asked the Lord to step into Ajayi's life as shots rang out in the back alley. "He's someone's son, Lord, and your creation," he remembered saying.

Further, that day from last week, the sound of sirens and flashing blue lights made him feel a little more at ease, coupled with the stillness of the young boy's departure. Pastor Briggs had remained on his knees in the prostrate position another twenty minutes or so in intimate prayer with the God of heaven. Afterwards, he got up and peered out the window. The porch was empty, but something was out of place. The third black milk crate from the top was sitting at an angle, crooked from the rest. The winter air rushed into the kitchen as he opened the back door. Pastor Briggs went out and looked up and down the alley. To the east was several police cruisers, officers, and a canine all surrounding Tamika's son, Shannon.

Pastor Briggs remained in deep thought about this incident for some reason: Shannon and another young man laid bent over the front hood of a Norfolk police cruiser with their hands on their heads. The young man used to attend the church, he recalled, not because he wanted to, rather the juvenile court system offered him an alternative sentencing to juvenile prison: six straight Sundays attending and helping out in the church. It posed a rehabilitative way to repay society for the bad choices he had made. The then fourteen-year old lasted two weeks before breaking curfew, at which time he was sent away to juvenile prison for three months.

"Dear Lord. Please intervene," Pastor Briggs recalled uttering as he had turned back towards the porch. The fact that the crates had been moved wouldn't allow him to walk past the stack without checking them. He recalled having taken a small plastic grocery bag from inside the church to potentially use for the contents of the crates. The other five grocery sacks were filled with water bottles, ready for recycling.

Still reminiscing on events that happened the previous week, Pastor Briggs recalled unstacking the crates, and the clear empty bottles lay lopsided as if something were causing them to rest unevenly. Curiously, he removed the top half of them and stopped at what appeared to be a black object in the shape of a handgun. Pastor Briggs looked over his shoulder back towards the alley, then back down into the crate. He removed the black handgun while thinking, "Jesus!" This event from the previous week laid so heavily upon his heart, but a visitor would now snap him up from memory lane.

"Pastor......Pastor," unsuspecting and deep in thought, the voice fell on deaf ears.

"Hey, Pastor!" a woman's voice sounded, snatching him from his thoughts. A glance over at the sidewalk leading into the church's parking lot revealed Sister Evans, a sixty-year old retired school- teacher, whom was also a part of the worship team. Sister Evans took care of the small things that often were looked over, like making sure the children's coats were zipped up before stepping out into the winter air or sending holiday cards to all the members. Pastor Briggs was never without thanks and praise for her. He was often sure to encourage Sister Evans assuring her that the Lord sees her efforts behind the scenes but that her rewards shall be visible to all.

"Sister Evans, what brings you around so early?" he inquired with a warm welcoming smile.

"Well, it ain't like I got a lot to do away from the church, pastor," she informed him while starting to laugh at the truth of her statement. Shaking the snow from her pullover snow boots." And besides, I thought you'd like some of my hot chocolate with marshmallows." Scanning her surroundings, she held up a dark green canteen with a silver cup attachment.

"Why thank you, Sister! I'll be right with you, just let me gather my things here."

"Oh, I'm sorry Pastor! Let me help you," she said stepping back off the church's front porch.

"No! No! This will only take a second. Why don't you go on in the church and get warm? I'll be right in. My office door is open," he informed her kindly.

Pastor Briggs spent a few more moments marinating on his thoughts while gathering up the signage and letters. Then he ditched the frigid air for a warmer climate inside the church where Sister Evans was doing what she did best, preparing her irresistible hot chocolate.

Twenty minutes later the two sat inside his first-floor office sipping on hot chocolate with marshmallows dissolving slowly on top of the hot liquid. "Wow, this is really good, Sister!"

"Thanks, and pastor if you don't mind me asking, what were you in such deep thought about as I rounded the corner? I called out your name twice before you even answered." Sister Evans stood and leaned over the highly polished wood desk and refilled both their cups.

"Well I do apologize. I wasn't trying to ignore you," he reconciled.

"I know, I know, sir. I was just wondering that's all."

"Really, I'm glad you asked. About a week ago, a young man left this back in a milk crate on the back porch."

Miss Evans gasped at the sight of the weapon. "Dear Lord, help us!" she whispered.

"That's not all. I think that Shannon, Tamika's son, may have been involved in something, but I'm not sure what." Pastor Briggs tapped on the keys of his laptop in front of him. Taking the moment to send a reply message to a fellow pastor who asked if he would make a guest appearance next Sunday at the church in the metro.

"It's so sad with all the young lives being lost nowadays. It must be something in the baby's formula they're drinking these days," Sister Evans joked, sipping from her cup as Pastor Briggs chuckled.

"You're probably right on that, Sister."

She was rocking back and forth calmly, still in shock at the weapon now in the pastor's front drawer.

Pastor Briggs straightened his blue tie lying flat against his shirt. "Remember Sister, it's not flesh or blood we're at war with. The problem is with principalities and powers. You know the rest! Ephesians 6:1, that's when the Bible tells us to wear God's armor."

"Yes pastor, wear the armor, but I tell you that I use my shield of faith probably more than anything."

The pastor laughed. "Well how 'bout you use some of that faith and pour me another cup of your good ol' hot chocolate."

Without hesitation she honored the request made by the servant of God. "Have you talked to Tamika?"

"No! Like I mentioned, I'm not sure if her son is involved in anything. None-the-less, it does seem somewhat ironic that the same day the young man stashed the weapon on church grounds, Shannon was detained by Norfolk's finest."

"Hold on, didn't Shannon get into some trouble a few years back? Sister Evans asked." She began putting on her coat and gloves.

Avoiding the question, "Here, let me give you a ride home," the pastor offered, standing, reaching for his coat hanging on the coat rack behind him.

"No sir, you won't! The brief walk is what keeps me young, and besides, I only live a block from here, so sit back down, and let me get my exercise on. And as to my question about Shannon?"

"Yes ma'am! To answer your question, the young man spent a small amount of time in a confined space. Yes...he did find trouble."

"Well the good Lord needs to intervene, 'cause it's time for our community to get some relief, and we saints need to become proactive. Maybe, granted God's will, we can save some of these lives." She strolled over to his office door and stopped before exiting. Pastor Briggs was staring out the window past the quaint snowflakes falling. His gaze was upon the next generation, two young black males standing at the bus stop. One with long dreads, bobbing his head as if it was easily noticeable that he was listening to music from a wireless headset. The other young man stood beside him holding a black skateboard and talking to someone on his phone. Both looked to be in their early teens and not concerned with the police's presence.

"Pastor Briggs, are you okay?" she asked still standing in the doorway observing his demeanor.

"Yes! I'm sorry, I thought you had left, Sister! I'm just standing here realizing that I'm going to get involved. Yes, that's what I plan to do, get involved."

Chapter 4

Psalm 1:1

On a Wednesday morning, "Boy, get yo' butt up. Shannon! Shannon!" Tamika yelled outside her son's bedroom door. "I got something for that!" Tamika said under her breath just before dashing into the kitchen. After removing a knife from the utensil drawer, Tamika b-lined back to her son's door and ripped the black and white sign hanging by a string from his door: "Business in progress." Tamika wedged the butter knife tip in between the door and latch. With a couple of hard jerks and wiggles, the door popped open.

"Momma!" Shannon yelled pulling the sheet over his naked mid-section.

"Cynthia?... What are you doing in my house in the damn bed with my son?" Tamika asked the girl angrily.

Sitting half naked beside her son with her legs pulled tight to her chest, "I'm so sorry Mrs. White!"

"Mama, why are you breaking into my space?" he asked feeling a little bit embarrassed as he leaned off the bed to grab a pair of gray sweatpants to slide into.

"Excuse me? When you start payin' the bills around here, then you'll have a say in this house. And you, young lady...you need to put your clothes on, and I'm calling your mom," she said before leaving to retrieve her phone from the coffee table in the living room.

About forty-five minutes later Shannon strolled out his front door disappointed that things didn't go like he wanted. "Dang, moms be trippin!" He thought looking back at the front door as he grabbed Cynthia's hand. Not taking any precautions, he checked to make sure a bullet was in the chamber of his .38, then he tucked it in his waistband and pulled his shirt over it. He went and scraped the ice off the windshield of his smoke gray 87' Grand National with a black rag top.

The car needed a motor, that's what the junkie whom sold it to him said just before Shannon gave him two zips for the keys and title. The young banger planned to have the car completely restored by the summer, but for now, it sat in his mom's driveway. It was 11:24 AM, and he was late for high school. The streets motivated him more than his education. A piece of paper stating that he made it through four years of public school wouldn't protect him from the ruthless street life he was used to. He became a 13th Street boy not for protection, rather he did it to belong. His dad was murdered in a street dice game, leaving his mom, Tamika, alone to raise a boy already tainted in the hood...a strong-willed hardheaded boy at that.

The idea of Jesus Christ and Christianity was boring to Shannon. His biased thinking was reinforced after spending those two long weekends with Pastor Briggs, forced to help him around the church. Still, with his mom's manufacturing job, they were living a little better than most. The big homies also gave him work to sell, money his mom sometimes questioned, but didn't really put up a fuss about. So instead of going to school, Shannon decided to go sell a little work

29

down on Earl Street and 14th. That's where Ajayi tried to jack him and the homie a week prior.

Shannon realized that if it hadn't been for that little girl riding her Big Wheel that he might not be alive. But more than that, he wondered if the prayers with that pastor on those boring Sunday's really worked, because that day, he saw the silver tip of the bullet inside the barrel of Ajayi's gun. The neighborhood Shannon lived in embraced diversity with families of all nationalities, like his next-door neighbor, Mrs. Chum. An old Asian woman, who owned and operated a takeout only Asian Style Deli. For blocks, each family's personality offered a look into different cultural views when it came to their contributions in the community, at least the ones who were unafraid of the wars between gangbangers.

Shannon walked along the sidewalk next to Haron Blvd keeping an eye out for police and his hand on the work, just in case he needed to get rid of it quickly. The pathway leading back to Earl Street was just ahead. He remembered laying on the hood of the police car and making eye contact with Ajayi as the cop walked into the very pathway he was now entering.

"Hey Shannon!" he heard a soft female voice calling out behind him. Her voice echoed amidst the traffic on Haron.

It was Anita Scolls. She waved at him from the platform of The North Street Haron Train Station. She was rocking a white, one-piece body suit by Acvoo. Shannon had always felt something for her. He jogged across Haron up onto the platform.

"What's good, ma?" greeted the dope boy, attempting charm.

"Nothing! 'Bout to go take this stupid test. Why you ain't in school?"

"Had to handle somthin'."

"Mm hmm... Let me find out you skippin' school just to shack up with one of these groupies." Anita casting doubt before starting to laugh flirtatiously. She wore big white and black shades that nearly covered half her face, but he still imagined her stunning hazel eyes behind them.

"Didn't know I held your interest like that, ma," he countered subtly inferring, suggestively staring at her ardently desiring she'd skip school and allow him to explore that bangin' body.

"Guess you gon' have to try a little harder, huh? You look cute though!" she challenged as he smiled deviously.

He was dressed in a dark burgundy, waist length Calvin Klein wind breaker with black and gray faded jeans to match. Shannon was a lady's man in every aspect with his inch- long burgundy tip dreads. Standing at six feet and light skinned, they loved how he towered over them. Anita was 5'3", and right then, she was candy eyed for the banger. Anita was a smart girl heading to Grambling the next semester on a full scholarship.

Suddenly, a tan two door 82' Buick Regal pulled up. "Westside Crip cuz," the passenger yelled then stuck a sawed-off twelve Gauge out the window pulling the trigger. Shannon jumped at the words Westside Crip, being affiliated and always alert. He reached for his strap as he dove onto the concrete, peripherally watching Anita. But the shot found and claimed her 5'3" frame lifting her spirit to glory and slamming her fragile body forcefully to the platform with a solid lifeless thud. The tires screeched as the '82 Regal peeled off. Her shades flew off her face on impact exposing the only cognizable correspondence from her now stunned rather than stunning hazel eyes, the question, "Why me, Lord?"

Chapter 5

Proverbs 8:27

It was seventeen degrees on a Friday morning. Ajayi was hoping the weather would change for the better before the birthday bash for Cuz, his homeboy that night. He drifted in and out of his thoughts sitting in his third period Language Arts class. To him, Ms. Collins was teaching in circles. Most of the stuff he'd heard back when he was in the tenth grade. So, in between texts with Tristan and Dana, his shorty on the side, Ajayi paid Ms. Collins no mind. Rather his mind was on texting. At this very moment with Tristan, specifically Tristan's wild, out of body experience which he was trying to convince everybody he had at the exact moment he was shot. But Tristan also tried to get Ajayi to come and hang out with him at the hospital to check out

"Pastor on Wheels," a program sponsored by the hospital where pastors are contracted to come onsite and spend time with patients.

The bell rang, ending the class session. Ajayi scooted away from his desk and read Dana's last text while walking towards the exit. Ajayi looked up intermittently, avoiding a collision with others, and that's when he saw them; two Norfolk Police officers standing at the classroom door. "Damn it's a good thing I ain't strapped, 'cause these fools looking right at me," he thought. "Maybe this is the reason I haven't been able to go back and get my tool, 'cause I would definitely be packing right now."

"Ajayi Cox?" a short, potbellied black officer asked.

"Yeah...what's good?" he responded hesitantly.

"You need to come with us, sir," the other officer of normal build instructed him as he reached and grabbed Ajayi's elbow with one hand and his backpack with the other.

Twenty-five minutes later, Ajayi sat with his left wrist handcuffed to a metal loop ring protruding from a metal table inside Interview room 6-B. The table and three chairs were the only objects in the room. The other two metal chairs were across the table in front of him. Behind the two chairs, built into the sheetrock wall, was a silver tinted two-way mirror, and Ajayi could feel the presence of someone on the other side watching him.

The fat officer had thoroughly searched Ajayi, taking all of his belongings, stating it was for his and their safety. Ajayi sat wondering what was so pressing that the police came and got him from school. After another five minutes or more, the door opened, and a very attractive white female with red hair weaved into a ponytail walked in carrying a black leather briefcase. She shut the door behind her without taking her eyes off Ajayi, then pulled a chair closer to the table and sat down. She placed the case on the table while still staring and yet not saying a word.

"Excuse me officer, do you mind telling me why I'm here?" Ajayi asked as she removed a folder from the briefcase and opened it before him.

"It's detective, not officer, and I'll be right with you," she stated, preoccupied. Minutes passed that seemed like hours before she stopped glancing at the documents in the folder and spoke again. "Okay. I'm Detective Mary Holder, and how are you, Mr. Cox?"

Ajayi suppressed the anger inside of him and decided to be smart about the situation instead of arrogant. "I haven't done anything wrong, and I know all my homeboys live by the code, snitches wear stitches!"

Dodging his statement, Detective Holder laid a photo in front of him. "Do you know her, Mr. Cox?" she asked while holding a finger up towards the two-way mirror.

Ajayi looked at a picture of a very beautiful sister of caramel skin and rich blonde dyed hair. She appeared to be about his age. "Nah! Who is she?"

Detective Holder leaned back in her chair while clearing her throat. "Look Ajayi, your homie spilled his guts. You've been implicated for the murder of Ms. Anita Scolls. So, get comfortable, Mr. Cox," Detective Holder informed him pointing at the picture laying on the table. So, you stay loyal, but your homies will be out on the street.

Her words slammed into Ajayi's chest like a ton of bricks. "Implicated?" he thought, "What was one of the homies doing snitching? Who was it?"

"Now, where were you on Wednesday morning between 9 and 11 AM? And don't lie to me because we also have an eye-witness." Detective Holder lied to the young thug just to shake him up, hoping he would break. The truth of the matter was that Ajayi's homeboys were in custody for the murder of Anita Scolls, but neither one was talking.

"Look, I was at school, check with whoever you need to, I ain't peel nobody's cap. You feel me!" Ajayi said confidently. And a shawty look like that, I ain't 'bout to forget. He had busted his gun numerous times before that moment and might have murdered a few innocent bystanders unknowingly, but Anita definitely wasn't one of them.

Detective Holder stood and kicked her chair backwards. The metal chair slammed into the sheetrock wall leaving a three-inch hole. "It's black thugs like you who run down your own neighborhoods causing innocent people like Ms. Scolls to lose their lives over your senseless acts and meaningless feuds."

The door to the interview room flew open. A uniformed police officer walked in with his hands resting on his utility belt. His right index finger tapped the butt of his Glock 40. Ajayi smirked at the sight of him, wondering if they were attempting to play good cop, bad cop. Detective

Holder's breath reeked as she stood hovering over the cool, calm, and collected teenager.

"You don't know anything about hood life, Miss Uppity! As a matter of fact, I want my lawyer," Ajayi said folding his arms across his chest.

Detective Holder stood upright and tugged at her jacket sleeves. She felt indigestion settling in. For years she had allowed street punks like the one in front of her to live in her head rent free. The fact that every one of them lived by a street code made her skin crawl. Both she and the Norfolk police officer left the room. Minutes later another black female officer poked her head into the room, then shocked him with her words after entering and unlocking the handcuffs.

"Okay you're free to go, please follow me!" The young rookie officer bit her bottom lip as Ajayi stood to his feet. The young banger was 5'10" in height with a chiseled physique. He put on his dark brown Jeffrey Rhodes leather coat with the white collar. Ajayi shook his pants, then looked at the officer. "After you," he gently offered, trying to peep her curves in uniform from the back. The way she looked at him, bit her bottom lip, and the way she sashayed as he walked behind her, clearly sent a message to him that she was choosing his thuggin' and was available. He thought to himself that the ride down the elevator was rewarding even more so when she handed him a piece of paper that read, "I'm down for whatever," listing her phone number, email, and shift hours.

Ajayi looked at her in a self-assuring way. An hour later, he hopped off the train down the street from North St. Station on the east side. He was taking a big risk, but when the tool man was popped by the feds on a shipment coming in from Port City, Savannah, Ajayi knew he needed to get to his own strap, but too much time had lapsed. Time wasn't on his side in that regard. This was supposed to be an easy and very quick temporary safe haven for his Glock Z3, now turning into a nightmare on Earl Street. But even worse, using one of his homeboy's straps or buying one from an unknown source on the street was asking for a body charge if he were caught with a burner.

Ajayi had entrusted the sanctity of the church with his tool, and it had paid off so far, but he hadn't quite put two and two together in realizing that being just a branch of the tree of living water would net him so much more in daily peace. So, his focus was on his piece instead. In his mind, he had created a real conundrum for himself, not easily remedied.

Chapter 6

Proverbs 8:4

This particular part of Haron Blvd. on the south end was known for producing some of the city's grimiest thugs. The streets were littered with empty beer cans, liquor bottles, and all around the dumpsters were used condoms, the evidence of hookers tricking with married men and women. The South End Train Station was next to Ray's Car Wash, which was a killing ground or what the locals called the South Haron Blvd. graveyard due to so many young lives abruptly taken in the confines of the car wash stalls. On the opposite side of the train station was Essence Strip Mall, home to Seven Mile Shop, an urban store founded by French Montana, the rap mogul built the mall and only hired young single mothers who's baby daddies caught bids and were now serving time upstate.

The rest of the mall housed six other quick shop stores, where young thugs hang out showing off their whips sitting on big boy rims! Then there's Freddie's, a social gathering place that serves spicy soul food and has a picnic style seating area. The train station and bus stop were packed with pedestrians walking to and from the station.

Again, with three blocks to walk off the main strip, the young thug put on a skull cap and headed to his destination. It was still early in the day, so most of the residents were still in the comfort of their homes. But it wasn't the average working American he was concerned about. It was the night walkers of the streets, whether it be the drug dealers or the crackheads. They were going to pull a jack move or represent their hood simply because Ajayi, a strange face, was in their cut. The crackheads would attempt a stick-up with whatever object enabled them with heart or they'd beg their way into a blast off the pipe.

The sky was gray now, and the wind was biting, sneaking into every crack possible to remind the thug it was still winter. Ajayi stepped off the sidewalk and onto Bronx

Street. Its name speaks for itself. Back in the sixties, New Yorkers immigrated down south to expand their mafia businesses and occupied residence in this particular neighborhood.

Thompson Middle School, with its mirror glass tinted windows, sat across the street on the right side. Kids waited on the side of the school in single file lines waiting for their buses to pull up to take them home. A Norfolk police officer casually strolled among the kids and school's staff members, providing a sense of safety, or at least that was the appearance. Ajayi could now see Earl Street.

Ajayi was a block away from the church. He looked to his right as a young black dude stepped out onto the porch of a mild green one-story house just as Ajayi stepped back onto the sidewalk after crossing Bronx Street. The young man was led by a big ol' red nosed pit bull. Sniffing its way around the front yard before finally urinating, creating a fresh yellow patch in the snow. Well, maybe not so fresh, but you know what I mean.

"Hurry up!" The dude angrily barked as his dog's urination seemed not to stop.

Both Ajayi and the young man-made eye contact briefly. To be in enemy territory without a strap was a very vulnerable point in a thug's life, yet he held his composure. It's been said that the eyes tend to speak what words cannot, and either you give respect or the opposite with them. Briefly glancing at someone was to acknowledge someone with benefit of the doubt, natural, mutual respect.

The church building's belfry came into skyline view. The black and brown shingles were starting to fall off. Work would have to be done with care soon on the old structure. Still, the belfry reached high into the sky, towering above the leafless snow-covered tree limbs.

He was now standing at the corner of 12th and Earl Street. A sign in the church's yard read 'Fragile forgiveness.' Ajayi shook his head as the memory of the old white guy rocking back and forth on his knees upright to a semi-prostrate position flooded his mind. Suddenly the front door opened, and the same white man walked out the door, to the mailbox. The man looked up to his left noticing Earl, then back right where he and Ajayi made eye contact, and it was warm and different.

The stare had nothing to do with intimidators sizing one another up. Strangely, their spirits connected instantly. Ajayi turned and walked left along a twelve-foot tall white cinder block wall stretching the whole block, with Earl Street painted in red on it. Sensing that the white dude was still eyeing him, he decided to walk past the alleyway and turn back up when the old man went back inside. Two black hearses rolled past Ajayi from behind. He immediately thought about Anita Scolls. The girl's murder produced undue trauma and grief for her family. The tragic infliction gripped at their souls. And the question remained, why?

The first hearse came to a stop at the stop sign, and the one behind it pumped its brakes until it fell in line behind the first one.

The white man was no longer there as Ajayi looked over his shoulder. So, he turned back heading for the alley and the back porch where his tool was stashed. Pastor Briggs knew right away, after seeing him, who the young black kid was. The stare in the young kid's eyes spoke of a tiredness in his soul, and it yearned for a rest that only God could provide. The moment their eyes locked, Pastor Briggs felt God drop in his spirit that Ajayi was going to be a new light within his ministry. The sanctuary was still, but alive with the presence of God.

Pastor Briggs moved down the aisle past the pews towards the pulpit, where he would enter into his office. Pastor Briggs removed the handgun from his desk drawer and left the office. Now in the kitchen, he waited for his guest. Ajayi stepped to the side as a heavy duty, Dodge Ram 3500 with its snowplow scraping the asphalt rolling passed him coming out of the alley. The black driver nodded his head at Ajayi then raised the plow before driving away for safety and precautionary measures.

Ajayi walked right past the sidewalk leading inside the church's backyard. He hadn't noticed the basketball court off to the right before, but the glass backboard, with an imprint of a cross etched into the glass, hastily drew his attention. Ajayi was impressed that someone had come up with such an idea. On the side of the church, parked between the exterior wall and basketball court, was a gray 90's style van with "Christ In All" in white letters printed on the side of it. His heartrate went up, but why, he wondered? Street life taught him never to fear, however the stare in the white man's eyes put him into at least a state of concern or confusion. It was welcoming, but, at the same time, an extension of something unrevealed. "What?" he thought.

Chapter 7

Proverbs 8:22

"What's he doing? Oh, right, maybe he's a "Jesus freak" now!" Detective Morrison mocked as they sat on their stakeout! The two decided to tail Ajayi in hopes of him leading them to something, even if it was a small piece of evidence in the murder case of Anita Scolls.

"Maybe we are wasting our time here. Word on the street is that the bloods have the drop on the gang responsible for the girl's murder already," Morrison continued, sipping on his caramel mocha.

"I don't know about all that, but we gotta stay with this. That was a senseless act, and as for your Jesus comment, we all have flaws. I need the blood myself," Detective Holder said, laughing to herself.

"So, you're a naughty girl, huh?" Morrison asked.

"In your dreams, Morrison," she responded, "Look, the kid has potential, and I think with the right guidance, maybe he could be persuaded to do right," she said as they watched Ajayi step inside the church fence.

Everything looked quiet as Ajayi stepped onto the back porch. Anxiety set in as he noticed the crates had been moved. They were now stacked near the back tire of the bike. In the same order, but in a different place. Ajayi went and moved the top three crates and dug into the bottles.

"Looking for this?" The voice from behind him startled Ajayi, and instinctively, he reached towards his lumbar waist area for his tool. But nothing was there. The young banger dropped his head and thought, "*for real?*"

Ajayi stood and turned to face the white dude, the same guy he had seen weeks ago praying. The white dude was about his height with a slimmer build. His salt and pepper hair seemed to radiate. Both men looked in the alley as a blunt orange SRT Charger sped up the alleyway. The windows were up and tinted black, the bass pounding inside the performance car, vibrated inside Ajayi's chest.

Pastor Briggs noticed a change in Ajayi's demeanor, a readiness for whatever.

"Don't worry, there is a hedge of protection around you. How many times has death come near you, yet here you stand!" he said to Ajayi.

Ajayi looked at his gun in the man's hand, then back into the eyes of the man in possession of his "protection."

"First off, I ain't worried about nothing, you feel me? Secondly, you need to give me my piece and I'll be on my way," Ajayi said, stepping close to the stranger in an intimidating way.

"My name is Pastor Briggs, and yours?"

Ajayi couldn't believe it, the white dude was trying him. Street code and regulations stated such people had to be dealt with. His homeboys would label him soft if he didn't do anything. Ajayi looked over his shoulder. Pastor Briggs walked off the back porch and turned looking at the peeling paint and build of the snow around the bottom of the walls of the church.

"You know this place could use a touch up. What do you think?" The pastor then went and stood in the doorway. "I'll tell you what… there are only a few weeks before spring kicks in, come help me around here, and maybe I will give you your gun back, which I know you have a permit for, right?"

Ajayi cleared his throat. He was having one of those moments, where the good angel sat on his right shoulder, and a demon sat on his left. Both were whispering in either ear telling him what he should do.

"You see that camera there?" Pastor Briggs pointed to a shiny lens attached to its black housing mounted on the corner to their left. In fact, the camera was aimed directly where Ajayi had been crouched weeks earlier. "It continuously records without interruptions. What's your name son?"

Ajayi hesitated.

"Look, let God help you. There is a reason for our encounter, or I could turn in the footage, along with the illegal weapon, over to the proper authorities."

Ajayi thought back to when he raised the strap, trying to fire the weapon blindly. Still the young thug didn't say a word.

"I'm here pretty much every day, so stop in when you have made a decision." Pastor Briggs turned to walk away.

"Man, you don't know what these streets are like," Ajayi said motioning with his hands.

Pastor Briggs turned back around in the middle of the doorway, "You'd be surprised who you're talking to. You see it's Jesus who fights my battles, he's working for you too. I'm sorry, what is your name?"

"Ajayi," the young banger said reluctantly.

"It's very nice to meet you, Ajayi." Pastor Briggs went to close the church doors but stopped. "I'd like to extend another offer to you. Saturday and Sunday church services start at 11 AM." The pastor then closed the door, leaving Ajayi wondering.

Chapter 8

Psalm 103:4

I t was still Friday afternoon, and Shannon paced back and forth in Prodigy's basement. "Aye, bruh. You keep interrupting our game of Madden, bruh. We 'bout to pull up on them fools tonight at ol' boy's party. We gon' handle that," Lil Fab reassured his big homie.

"My bad fam, just thinking, maybe, I could have done something different, you feel me?" Shannon sat down on top of a pool table and started breaking down a cigar.

"Aye, as long as I been banging, ain't nobody been able to stop no bullet, bruh," Lil Fab lifted his spirit.

"Now, that's real spit," Shannon acknowledged.

"You just got made, stupid," Prodigy said, pausing the Play Station.

Lil Fab shrunk back into the leather cushion. "Why you always gotta put people on blast?" he asked, unpausing the game console.

"Look, both of y'all fall back, and Lil Fab, you did just come onto the set. You check your strap yet? 'Cause this here is about some get back, you feel me?"

"Man, I stay ready to put in work. Just so you know, these tear drops tattooed under my left eye ain't for nothing."

Prodigy laughed, "Okay, what's all the other tats for? You got like ten or eleven tats on your face, bruh. I would hate to be you in an interview," Prodigy said, shaking his head.

Shannon and Lil Fab weren't quite as well off as Prodigy, the 6'3" shooting guard for Central High School, who had already committed to the University of Florida. Prodigy's mom and dad worked as civil attorneys and had given their son everything he ever wanted. Lil Fab, on the other hand, was just fourteen, and lived in the housing projects a block away, near Haron and Lake Street. The young killer was very shy and insecure growing up until he was approached by some 13th St OG who painted a picture for the teenager. They sold him the dream of becoming a family with their set in return for his loyalty and committing evil acts. Lil Fab's mama, Big Shirley, a heroin addict is constantly nodding out or bringing tricks into their tiny apartment to support her habit. Lil Fab's dad was sentenced to life for the murder of a Norfolk police officer.

Lil Fab jumped to his feet. "I really feel like you trying me, bruh." He stopped hovering over Prodigy.

"Both of ya'll chill, and get focused on the business at hand," Shannon said, impressing upon them the tragic day Anita's wings were clipped forever.

Prodigy, the natural athlete, stood to his feet, slinging the wireless controller down behind him. "Aye, my bad, lil man. I'ma go get dressed," he said walking past Lil Fab who stood at 5'4."

Shannon walked within inches of Lil Fab's face. He handed the little homie the cigar.

"It's in and out, you got that? Get out of the car, go inside the house, handle your business, and get out."

"Yeah, we been over this already fam," Lil Fab reminded Shannon.

Shannon could see the eagerness in Lil Fab's eyes. It reminded him of putting in work for the set. He placed a hand on Fab's shoulder, "This gon' put some hype on your name in the street baby, you feel me? It's about respect. Can't nobody come in the hood disrespecting our turf, aight? Especially taking an innocent life."

Lil Fab blew gray smoke into the air, "Aight," he responded.

Chapter 9

Psalm 103:12

The time was 9:15 PM on this Friday night as Ajayi stood looking out over the city. The lights atop the skyscrapers blinked simultaneously, alerting pilots to beware of the city's skyscrapers. The pastor from earlier today saw him, and quite frankly, Ajayi didn't know how to resolve the situation. After all, we're talking about a man of God, and Ajayi remembered a sermon he heard before, "Touch not my anointed." He did know, though that the man of God meant the Lord's business and that he wouldn't be getting his Glock back anytime soon. So, he felt that his only option was to borrow a gun from one of his peeps, however risky that may be.

"What's up with that hundred zipper, Michael Jackson leather jacket? You going to Cuz's birthday party or a thriller concert?" Tristan asked from his hospital bed.

Ajayi looked his jacket over as he turned to face his friend. Tristan laughed out loud, then clutched his stomach.

"Come on man, you're hurting me here," Tristan said as both friends laughed together.

Ajayi looked at the Bible beside his friend's bed.

"You trippin' fam. All of a sudden, you trust in God, huh?" Ajayi asked.

Tristan's hospital room was a typical recovery room. A heart monitor machine was tucked in the corner between his bed and the bathroom doors. Tristan's half eaten dinner tray sat uncovered on the mobile tray cart next to his bed. Ajayi sat down in the chair off to the right at the end of the bed.

"Yeah, as a matter of fact, I'm clinging to the cross," Tristan said, sitting up in bed. "I had an out of body experience, bruh."

"Get out of here fool, that stuff only happens on TV," Ajayi said.

"Real talk! The moment I was shot, I left my body. I stood up while lying there on the sidewalk, looking down at myself. I seen the blood pouring from my stomach! I remember when ole boy was taking my shoes off then unclipped my phone from my side."

Ajayi couldn't believe it. "You clinging to the cross, what does that mean?"

Tristan grabbed his Bible.

"Come on man, I ain't got time for this," Ajayi said, standing to his feet.

"Nah, bruh, the streets can wait. I just shared a life changing moment with you. Can I get twenty minutes?" Tristan asked.

Ajayi sighed heavily and then took his seat again.

"Thank you!" Tristan said, then flipped to Colossians 2:11-14 and began reading.

"Blotting out the handwriting of ordinances that was against us, which was contrary to us and took it out of the way, nailing it to his cross."

The look on Ajayi's face asked Tristan to explain.

"Basically, what the Word of Life is saying is that God saved me from dying in my sins by dying on the cross for me, long before I got shot. I'm done, Ajayi. I'm done with the banging and the street life altogether. I've asked God to prune me like a tree for new growth, and a part of that process is to become what I've never been. I want to become that tree deeply rooted by living water so that a fountain can spring up within me that I may never thirst again. You should want the same. Listen, I know it sounds silly, but Jesus says in John 16:14, "But whoever drinks the water that I shall give him will never thirst. But the water that I shall give him will become in him a fountain of water springing up into everlasting life."

And in John 15:2, he says, "Every branch in me that does not bear fruit, he (his father) takes away; and every branch that bears fruit, he prunes, that it may bear more fruit. You my boy, Ajayi, and I care ab..."interrupted by the nurse.

Tristan's hospital room door eased open, and a short, heavy-set white nurse came in.

"Sorry, but visiting hours are over," she told them.

Ajayi looked down at his phone. It was 9:50 PM. The nurse removed a clear clipboard from the head of Tristan's bed.

"Aight man, seems like you got it all figured out. Hope that works out for you, my homie. I'ma ride out, hit this party," Ajayi said, dapping his friend up. Ajayi stopped by one of his homies and borrowed a 9mm for some insurance before heading out to Cuz's.

Notorious BIG's "One More Chance" pounded from the house's speakers as Ajayi rounded the corner of Edmund and Dale. The temperature was forty-five degrees now, maybe a bit warmer, making it cozy in a sense. Cuz's front yard was packed with his friends from high school, mostly his football team. The varsity basketball team was there also. Cuz was an overweight kid from Brooklyn, who was half black and half Puerto Rican. Even though he was 5'10" with a protruding belly, the girls liked him, because he carried himself well, dressing in Gucci and Coach, day in and day out. Cuz, with his curly hair, was "the work man," trafficking cocaine back and forth with his uncle from New York to Norfolk. Tonight, wasn't any different. Cuz stood in a dark blue Gucci jumpsuit with matching suede loafers, watching Art, his tan-nosed, eight-month old pit bull chase his girlfriend Sofie around.

"I told you he just playing. Stop running," Cuz said laughing.

"Get him!" Sofie cried out.

Ajayi scoped out some of his homies right away. In gatherings like this one, it was vital to do so. The cream-colored house with its black shutters, was two-stories with wild teenagers hanging from windows and crowding the front and back doors. Gang members stood on point with straps in hand. The house was semi-dark except for the disco light reflecting a red glow from the red bulbs replacing the normal white bulbs.

Ajayi adjusted the pistol he'd borrowed from one of the homies as he stepped through the fence opening into Cuz's yard. Art let out a bark, then ran over and sniffed Ajayi's hand, as the young banger bent over to pet him. Sofie sprinted over and jumped in Cuz's white Range Rover.

"What's good, son?" Cuz asked in his Brooklyn accent.

"Ain't nothing. Tryna get to where you at," Ajayi said, laughing to himself.

"Go get it, that's all I can say!" Cuz responded back.

Ajayi mingled with everybody as the night went on. Around 11:30 PM the blunt orange SRT Charger crept up Dale St. with the music on mute. Ajayi and his friends were hanging out back by the above ground swimming pool in the center of Cuz's backyard. Drake's "I'm so Proud of You" saturated the backyard, as the DJ wished Cuz a happy birthday.

"I wanna wish the birthday boy a happy birthday and many more. Let's raise our cups in a toast," the DJ instructed.

Everybody raised their disposable, blue plastic cups.

"Happy birthday, baby!" Ajayi said, handing Cuz a stack of money.

"Nah, man. That's dog food money, lil homie," Cuz responded, laughing as he reached under the glass patio table to retrieve a leather duffle bag. He unzipped it, revealing stacks of hundred-dollar bills.

"My dude, why you flexin' with all this paper like that?" Ajayi asked.

"It's my lifestyle, my man. In my world, it's all about stuntin," Cuz told him. Right on cue, Drake's "Started from the Bottom" blared from the speakers. "You see ol' boy right there?" Cuz asked, pointing at Darius.

Ajayi had seen the tall, braid-wearing kid before, but never really kicked it with him. Darius was taller than everybody at 6'6". He was a star on the basketball team and a star in the street game. Known as a ruthless killer, or as he liked to be called, "The Enforcer," Darius had been misguided most of his life by family members living thugged out lifestyles, and the negative effects had both dehumanized and demonized Darius. NBA scouts all lined the stands at his games at home and away. Still, evil darkened and pulled rigorously at his heart.

"Yeah, I seen him around, heard about the fire on the basketball court," Ajayi said while enjoying his hot wings. Art sat at attention at his feet, hoping for a bone.

"Go inside!" Cuz ordered the puppy. Art did as he was told and went into his customized doghouse. Cuz leaned over and whispered in Ajayi's ear, "He's the one who had the drop on Shannon but shot o' girl instead."

Chapter 10

Genesis 4:9-10

Lil Fab checked the double sawed off shotgun, as Prodigy turned onto Dale Street. The streetlight shone through the sunroof's perimeter reflecting off the plastic gear shifter in the center console. All three gang bangers were forced to protect against the blinding light. The music was on mute as they were out for revenge. Their rival's house came into view.

"Remember what I told you back in the basement," Shannon said, looking over his shoulder.

Wet snowflakes rested on the windshield as Prodigy pulled over to the curb one house down from Cuz's front door. A few stragglers from the party were on the front porch. Lil Fab pulled the blue dickie cap down to where it covered half his face. He opened the back door and got out.

No one really paid him any attention as he walked up the steps right into the house. The color red glowing from the bulbs helped to highlight his sect while concealing his identity as the young killer searched for his victim. Sofie stood at the refreshment table filling a plate with an assortment of fruits. She looked up and saw dark pupils as she made eye contact with Lil Fab. She watched him walk through the plastic doors and followed him, watching with the plate still in her hand.

As the dude unveiled a black shotgun, she dropped the plate to the cream colored 1X1 tile floor and put her hands to her mouth as he raised the shotgun to Darius' head without hesitation, pulling the trigger. Darius' body bounced off the above ground pool wall. Pandemonium broke out as the party goers screamed, running in all different directions. Ajayi instinctively untucked and raised his strap, firing at Lil Fab who dodged behind the pool. The bullet hit the pool wall causing a rush of water towards Ajayi and his homeboy.

Lil Fab hopped over the back fence and sprinted up the alley where his homeboys were waiting in the getaway car. He hopped in, and they peeled off. Art jetted from the deck into the alley, chasing the shooter. Ajayi and Cuz watched

Darius's body twitch, and then stop as he died, giving up the ghost.

Chapter 11

1 John 3:8

Detective Holder rested her neck on the rim of her tub and popped the rainbow transparent bubbles with her fingers. This was what she called some much-needed downtime and relaxation. The week had been an especially trying one indeed. Chasing down every tip in hopes of getting a lead in the murder case of Anita, among many in the city. She brushed a strand of her natural red hair from her right eye and again thought about the nice-looking kid she recently interviewed.

"Why do they commit such violent acts?" Detective Holder pondered, as she had for years now, ever since she stood within the perimeter of yellow tape at her very first crime scene. Her rookie year as a detective brought reality from obscurity to light in the cringe worthy dark and gruesome world of gang banging. Just hours after receiving her gold shield, she and her first partner, Detective Banks, were baptized on her first ever homicide investigation. The murder took place at the Franklin Gas Station right on the freeway off-ramp to downtown Norfolk. Eight-year old Janelle Robinson was shot in the head as she was playing a game on her iPad in the back of her dad's 89 baby blue Cadillac Fleetwood.

Witnesses saw a young black guy walk out of the gas station's front door wearing a bright red bandana tied on his right arm and seconds later, another young man wearing red followed. The gun fire lasted two minutes, but the life of Janelle would be lost forever, a lifetime void for her family. Over the years, Detective Holder found that, having studied murders intently, the one thing that stuck out was how volatile gang bangers could be. She also found that most just need to be noticed or loved. Detective Holder came from a lineage of police veterans. Her dad's dad was chief of police while her dad too was a homicide Detective. Her mom was aware of the risk, senseless violence, and the aftermath of the violence on the world outside their home. Thanks mostly to her husband and the evening news.

Motivated by these factors, Detective Holder was homeschooled up until her freshman year in high school. She enjoyed time with her mom throughout the years, receiving her curriculum, tests, and books by mail. She would study hard every morning and be rewarded for her efforts during the afternoon when she would play with her dolls and have tea parties with her mom.

Suddenly, her thoughts were interrupted by the ringing of her phone. The caller ID revealed that it was her partner, Detective Morrison. "You sure know how to pick your timing," she uttered sarcastically.

Morrison chuckled.

"Strap' em on Holder, we got a live one."

Thirty minutes later, Detective Holder stood over the body of Darius Hall. As his carcass lay sprawled out, the snow was compressed with his NBA formerly promising 6'6" dead weight and stained with his chilled blood.

"Witnesses said a short guy with a born complexion walked up to him, firing a single shot from a black rifle, then jumped over that back fence escaping into the night."

Holder knelt down on one knee, examining the latest murder victim. "Guess who's here?" Morrison pointed inside the house.

"Take him downtown." Holder ordered.

Ajayi sat in the same interview room, at the same table, staring at the same two-way glass. He had been in this position for an hour now. The sight of Darius' body on the ground told him that death could be around the corner and that o' boy could have easily shot and killed him instead. Pastor Briggs' words echoed in his mind, that he was protected. But why? With all the sins he committed, how could God protect or forgive him for that matter? Was he God's example of what was so amazing about grace or simply a fluke, a delayed case of the inevitable, grimly reaping what you sow?

The door clicked as the red headed woman walked in again. "You know, I was in chill mode before getting the call about your homeboy's murder, sorry this happened," she said scooting her chair up to the table. Detective Holder pushed the cup of hot chocolate over to Ajayi. "Here, thought you might want this."

"I'm straight. Why am I here?"

"Don't you want us to catch the guy who did this?" She blew, then sipped her coffee.

Ajayi only stared at her.

She leaned forward with both elbows on the metal table. "Okay, I think we got off on the wrong foot last time. I apologize for my comments about black people, don't you want better for yourself?"

"White people! Y'all live in this fantasy world like life is all peaches and cream. You have no idea of what it's like being a young black man in America. Yeah, Obama was our president, but that still doesn't change the racism. It doesn't change the fact that black men are still getting killed by police, unprovoked."

"People are going to be people, unique individuals, you can't let that determine your response. In fact, that's the only thing that you can control in any situation, how you choose to respond, how you choose to deal with adversity," Detective Holder said with concern in her eyes. "It was once told to me, if you don't like your life, then do something to make it better. You want to tell me what happened last night?"

Ajayi shook his head, "No," slowly.

Chapter 12

Malachi 4:5-6

T amika fastened the cap to the back of her earring as she walked into Shannon's bedroom. "Why is this child so messy?" she thought. Her son left early with friends and would meet her at the funeral home for Anita Scolls' funeral. Tamika needed a squeeze of Shannon's hand lotion until she could go shopping for household items later. It was Saturday morning, and services like this were recurring events for the weekend during the past month. After a few squirts into the palm of her hand, she rubbed her hands together then applied the lotion to her legs. While sitting on Shannon's bed, out of her peripheral vision, she saw a gold wrapper, a used condom. Tamika reached over the red comforter and raked it into the trash can next to his door, unconcerned. But what she saw behind the trash can stopped her in her tracks, an eight ball.

Pastor Briggs stood at the entrance of "Christ in All" church, greeting the mourners. Anita's murder was high profile. So, media vans aligned the curbs., although reporters were not allowed in the service. It was his job to bring the eulogy and protect the privacy of the families involved. Pastor Briggs had been fasting for a couple of days now, beseeching the Lord for guidance on what to deliver to the family and friends for consolation and honor to the young life that ended too soon. The words of the speech would be sensitive to the troubled hearts, but Pastor Briggs was okay with the words God had planted in his spirit.

"God bless you, thank you for coming." He welcomed an old couple. Shannon picked a couple of lint balls from his silky black Bally's sweater. Tamika threw the eight ball of cocaine into her son's lap.

"You need to straighten your face or get out my house! I don't want that evil stuff in my house." Shannon calmly handed the yayo to Felicia and refocused his attention on his three-hundred-dollar silk shirt.

Pastor Briggs walked down the aisle towards the pulpit but stopped at the sight of Tamika hurriedly walking past him in the opposite direction. "Hey!" he said stopping as she walked by.

"Hey pastor, how are you?"

"I'm fine, but I can see you're not, wanna talk?" she looked over his shoulder at her son, who was now on his phone.

"Yeah, guess I do."

"Okay, I got ten minutes. Let's go to my office."

After a short walk, Tamika took a seat on the wine colored, leather chair across from the pastor's desk. Pastor Briggs' chair squeaked as he leaned backwards. "Sorry, I been meaning to grease the ball bearings on this thing. What's the problem sister?"

"I know you remember my son from the work the court ordered him to do as punishment a while back."

"Of course. Unfortunately, he chose to renege on the deal sending him away for a short period," Pastor Briggs said, checking the time on his laptop: Sunday 10:50 AM. The service would start at 11:00 AM.

"He hadn't learned anything. Just the other week, I caught him with a young lady laid up in my house. And just before I arrived this morning, I found crack cocaine in his room, way too much for personal use. I think he sells that poison, and on top of that, he's into banging hard core. He wears red, his comforter is red. Everything he says, or thinks is red. And that old car in my driveway, he tied a red bandanna on top of the antenna, our house has been shot up because of his mess."

The Lord alerted Pastor Briggs' spirit about Shannon just as he had about Ajayi. Both young men, blue and red, were now a part of his ministry, and the pastor wouldn't be able to rest until he obeyed the voice of God. "I'll have a talk with him."

"Thank you so much." At 11:05 AM, Pastor Briggs removed the purple cloth, covering a four foot by three-foot picture of Anita. Her beautiful hazel eyes in the oversized photo commanded everybody's heart to weep tears salted with confusion, shock, pain, sorrow and mystery, but infused with joy and privilege.

Pastor Briggs draped his arm and robe around the shoulder of her best friend, Coco, then opened with scripture, Matthew 1:7.

"But if we walk in the light as He is in the light, we have fellowship one with another, and the blood of Jesus Christ, His son cleanseth us from all sin." He wanted to set the tone, focusing on life rather than death.

Shannon's phone vibrated; it was Lil Fab. Shannon excused himself and stepped out front on the sidewalk. "What's good fam?"

"Them people rode down on me last night." Lil Fab informed the big homie about Detective Holder and her partner questioning him for two hours the previous night.

"Aight, if they had something, they wouldn't have let you go," Shannon, the young killer rationalized. "Anyway, you did trash that missile though! Right?" he asked Lil Fab.

"Yup. It's wrapped tight on the bottom of Lake Flaying."

"Look, I'ma get up with you later-on today."

"Bet," Lil Fab said before hanging up.

Back inside, Shannon sat and listened to the rest of the eulogy. He stared at Anita's casket mostly, realizing and pondering it could have easily been him in her place. A little while later, the service ended. Pastor Briggs eyed Shannon as he shook hands with the long line of attendees. Tamika walked behind her son, purposely lagging behind so the pastor could have some one on one time with her son.

Pastor Briggs excused himself from the line and approached Shannon. "How are you?" he asked the young man.

"Hanging in there, sir, I guess. Just wish things could've been different, better for her. Why her and not me? But at least she's free now, without having to live in this chaotic world, a synthetic, cruel and crude knock-off of real life, no more. I just hope she's in a much better place on the other side, ya know?" Shannon passionately stated, reaching deep within at the roots and holding on to a branch of a tree fed by a river of tears.

"It's not as bad as you think son. God is in control. Hey, I was wondering if you wanted to finish helping out around here? Spring is in the air, and I could use some help painting on the exterior, and besides, I've never heard you talk like that. It seems you could use a drink from the fountain of living water."

Shannon stood thinking, intrigued by Pastor Briggs' offer.

"I have to agree with him. I really felt how you feel Shannon, and I think it's a good idea." Tamika said rambling through her purse. She then nervously looked back and forth between the two men.

"Okay, maybe I will sir, I'll let you know."

Tamika smiled and whispered, "Thank you...you can tell he's worth saving," as they walked past the pastor.

Chapter 13

Matthew 5:7

Ajayi zipped up his Idris Elba sport bomber as he sat in the front passenger seat of Cuz's two toned, black on gray 1969 Camaro SS 350/300 HP. "You ready?" he asked Ajayi as he pulled away from the curb.

"I stay down homie." The murder of Darius in Cuz's backyard wasn't just disrespectful, it brought heat to Cuz's multi-million-dollar drug ring. The mob bosses insisted that it be Cuz who sends the message about interfering with big money. Many up and coming go-getters offered their services, some even free of charge. It wasn't about the money in a high-profile case like this one. Getting your name out there as the one who resolved the situation meant respect, potential, more and bigger contacts down the road. And since it was Cuz's money, backyard and connection upstate whose concerns spoke volumes, the drug dealer decided it was time for him to bust his gun.

The street was dry from the salt and spring like weather with the constant beam of the noon sun. So, the Pirelli tires gripped the corner at twenty mph at which time Christ in All came into view.

"They just letting out too," Ajayi said checking his cellphone. Suddenly, a tugging started within Ajay. The pastor's face flashed across his mind. Ajayi shook the image though. He looked over at Big Cuz, and saw a concentrated, ominous look on his friend's face that he had never seen before. Point blank, it was downright evil.

Shannon walked along the sidewalk with Felicia, instructing the young lady where to deliver the eight ball. The low thumping of music from behind caused him to peep over his shoulder slightly, and his street instincts guided his arms in pulling Felicia between him and the street. Shannon grabbed his strap and let it hang beside him as he watched from his periphery. Cuz held the Mac-10 out of his driver side window and pulled the trigger. The back window of a red and black Ford Explorer exploded as the bullets came close to Shannon and Felicia, "Get down," he yelled.

Church attendees screamed and scattered, retreating back into church, and down the block away from the gun fire. Pastor Briggs ran and pulled Tamika by her elbow as she screamed and reached towards her son who was halfway down the block in front of her. Shannon was crouched low, face first in the snow drift. The bullets sounded like hard raindrops slamming on top of a metal tin roof, and then it stopped.

Anita's mother collapsed in the doorway leading back into the church. Tears streamed down her face as she repeatedly asked, "Why, Lord? Why?" The two-tone SS sped off, leaving a message, "Anytime, anyplace."

"Nooo, let me go, I gotta get my baby," Tamika yelled.

"He's fine! Stay in here," Pastor Briggs said leaving the foyer. Shannon dusted the snow from his pants, then helped Felicia to her feet.

"Is anyone hit?" the pastor asked as he jogged to the teenager's side.

"Nah! We straight! Aye, make sure she gets home, and do the same for my mom," Shannon said as he broke into a jog up Earl Street.

"Shannon! Shannon!" Pastor Briggs yelled but to no avail. "Dear Lord, help us," the man, of God whispered.

Later that night, Pastor Briggs prayed continually as he pulled into the parking lot at 2517 Webster Lane. He shifted his Chevy Malibu into gear and sat inside the confines of the cab for a moment. The events of that day saddened the heart of the man of God briefly, mainly feeling grief for the bereaved family. But the man of God quickly snapped out of it understanding that God allows situations in our lives as a test of our faith manifested in our reaction to them. After sitting with Anita's family another several hours in the sanctuary where all were quiet before the Lord, he excused himself to tend to a personal commitment that he made two years prior. A brother once told him years ago, "Take care of God's people, and the Lord will take care of you." So, Pastor Briggs had done just that.

The heavy gauged door clicked shut behind Briggs.

"Hey there pastor, nice to see you again."

"You too, Smitty. How's business?"

"You know, release one, in comes ten. Sign in right here sir," the raspy voiced man said.

Pastor Briggs did as he was ordered. The pastor remembered his own, not so distant, past and how he spent a few nights inside this very building years ago. God had always placed people in his life, planting seeds along the way, but it was his encounter with the Savior inside the cell that changed his perception and thoughts about Jesus Christ. On that night, the Lord came to the pastor in a dream. The then wide eyed, naive, young boy in Christ lived his life straddling the fence: in church with one leg and the strip clubs heavily planted with the other. In the dream, God gave him the vision of Paul's encounter of Christ on the road to Damascus: Acts 9:1-20. God told Pastor Briggs to also arise and preach the Gospel of Jesus Christ three consecutive times in a single night, which is exactly what he had done since that night.

The elevator doors opened just as they had over the years allowing the pastor and his escort to enter. A brief ride took them to the sixth floor where Pastor Briggs was led to the all-purpose room, and he was greeted by all thirty inmates with daps, hugs, and mainly big smiles. The Norfolk

County Jail accounted for a significant share of Christ in All ministries. It warmed the pastor's heart to encourage the men and women. Most embraced him, relating, because he too once wore the orange jumpsuit.

"Praise the Lord," he shouted. The room erupted with applause and shouts of praise.

Chapter 14

Numbers 24:9

Ajayi stood on his front porch, surveying the hood. It had been three weeks since the last incident between his set and the 13st boys. It was 1:30 PM, and with it having been a half day at school, he planned to spend a few hours with mom, taking in a late day movie. Lately, he had felt life and death situations tugging at him, and at times, with all the killings, it felt as though he didn't have long to live! Most of the snow had melted, revealing the matted salt, stained grass, and dirt: the not so majestic, clean and pure stage of a snowy, wintry wonderland. But the sun's rays shone brightly, streaming through scattered cumulus clouds.

Ajayi nodded his head at a silver Tahoe as it rolled past.

"Ajayi," called his mom through their screen door.

"Yeah, mama?" he answered walking back inside connecting with his mom through their open floor plan as she was removing the last of the dishes from the dishwasher. Alicia never liked to leave a messy kitchen, so the breakfast dishes had to be cleaned. "Ain't that your friends?" she asked, pointing at the 50" LCD flat screen.

Ajayi walked around to see who his mom was talking about. Two FBI agents, one on each side of Cuz, escorted him to an SUV with tinted windows in handcuffs! Headlines read, "BREAKING NEWS! Drug Kingpin of Norfolk linked to Upstate Mafia!"

"Damn Ajayi, baby, I knew there was something up with him, always pulling up in all those fancy cars! How many kids his age drive range rovers?" She asked toweling off her hands.

"That's because he was gettin' it, ma."

"He got it alright," she said walking to the back.

An hour later, they were traveling Hwy 10 East, heading to see Spiritual Vision, a movie starring Morgan Freeman as a preacher. Alicia exited the freeway in the suburbs of Southern Norfolk!

"I hope this ain't some boring, put me to sleep flick!" Ajayi said shifting in his seat.

"Boy watch yo' mouth, ain't nothing about God gon' be boring! You had better check yourself!" Alicia warned her son. She then turned right onto Snelling Ave, heading north into the small town of Roseville where the Roseville Cinema was located two miles ahead!

Ajayi studied the houses; most of them had nicely manicured lawns, decent cars and a familial aura about them! "How many of these dudes rep hoods out here?" he wondered, adjusting the strap in his waist.

"Ajayi baby, I've been thinking, maybe we should move out of the city! You know, a change of scenery. What do you think? I just don't want nobody, especially the police, knocking on my door at 2 AM talking about you getting shot or worse!"

He could hear the crackle in his mom's voice as she talked. He sighed and rolled his eyes her way. They had just had this same conversation, and he thought it was old. "Mama, can we enjoy ourselves and maybe talk about this later."

She shook her head affirmatively, because opening her mouth might cause tears to flow.

The foyer inside the cinema smelled of buttery popcorn, and except for a couple of movie goers the theater was empty. Ajayi and his mom maneuvered along the dark red velvet roped section of the six ticket registers. "Hi and welcome to Roseville Cinema, mates!" a high energy pigtail wearing short Australian female said with a land-down-under accent and a cheerful smile. "May I get you some goodies to fill your tummies?"

"Yes, thanks, I want some lemon heads, baked beans and a large buttered popcorn. Oh yeah, and a medium sprite," Ajayi's mom ordered. Ajayi placed his order as well, intrigued by the Australian accent and bubbliness of the young Aussie.

"Alrighty bloke and misses, just a few minutes, Next, may I entice you with some goodies?" and ten minutes later, they walked down the aisle with goodies to take their seats and enjoy the movie.

Unexpectedly, the overhead light flashed on, then Ajayi and his mom looked behind them because of the commotion brewing now in the area where they came in. Detective

Holder and her partner Morrison walked down the aisle, heading straight towards Ajayi. "You're under arrest in the suspected murder of Anita Scolls," Morrison said cuffing Ajayi.

"Nooo, what's going on?" Alicia asked in a panic, clutching her bucket of popcorn in one arm while trying to free her son from the detectives with the other. Detective Holder grabbed a hand full of Alicia's popcorn. She tossed a kernel or two into her mouth, then looked directly at Alicia with a smirk on her face.

"Please don't interfere with police work," she said to Alicia.

Now, take him to jail," Detective Holder ordered a uniformed officer.

Ajayi looked back at his mom with sorrow and frustration in his eyes as he was led up the aisle and out of the theater.

Chapter 15

Matthew 5:19.

The holding cell was packed and smelled of old dried pungent urine, while styrofoam cups were scattered all over the concrete floor. Ajayi sat on the same bench as a black homeless dude who was at the end, asleep, farting and snoring at the same time. The young banger wasn't concerned with the condition as much as the three Mexican dudes sizing him up on the bench in front of him. Six other black dudes were also in the tank, but they were preppy college kids, scared out of their minds. Ajayi, being the smart teenager, he was, he was able to adapt quickly. Having taken Spanish in school the previous year, he understood that the three Hispanics were talking about him. The tallest of them stood and walked over to where Ajayi sat. "I want your shoes, fool!" He said removing his shirt. The 6' 3" muscular Mexican was tatted up with the Mexican flag on his chest. His hair was pulled into a ponytail, and he had a mouth full of platinum.

Ajayi looked at his eight-hundred-dollar black Louis Vuitton boots then scooped the Mexican in front of him off his feet, slamming him headfirst into the concrete floor. With lightning speed, he got on top of the semi-conscious man, throwing punch after punch releasing anger that had built up in him over the past few weeks. Strangely, again Pastor Briggs flashed in his mind, but this time, he was standing next to a willow tree with its root system entrenched by a calmly flowing river, and this caused him to think back to what Tristan had said at the hospital about becoming a tree deeply rooted by living water.

The holding tank was in an uproar as guards rushed in as Ajayi almost caught a 187 just a few hours after being arrested. Ajayi was placed in a separate cell in solitary confinement.

"Man, how much is my bail?" Ajayi screamed from the segregated cell, across from the front booking desk.

A fat belly black guard with sergeant stripes waved his finger in the motion of no. "Sorry man, you would have made it upstairs to see the judge if it wasn't for your little episode fifteen minutes ago."

"What? The dude started with me." Ajayi yelled.

"Yeah well, you got the best of him," Sergeant Cooper said, walking over to the cell Ajayi was in. He said something into his walkie-talkie, and Ajayi's cell door popped open.

"C'mon, let's get you processed, after that, I'll show you your new home for tonight." They traded out Ajayi's clothes for a one-piece jump suit.

The elevator ride, up to the sixth floor was awkward. Sergeant Cooper read Ajayi's body language using the reflection of the stainless-steel wall next to the buttons running right through the basement.

"Hey, my man, this isn't a place to be. I've been working here twelve years, and I've seen young men like you get turned out. The floor you're going to is called the thunder floor. Admin assigned you to this floor because of your charges, and that fight earlier didn't help."

The double doors opened at the sound of a ding. A shiny clear coat of wax had the linoleum floor tile looking like someone had spilled water on it. Straight ahead was a control center with a single officer manning the floor. There was a 180-degree view to monitor all Pods.

Ajayi's orange shower shoes flapped as he followed the sergeant, "Cooper my man, brought some fresh meat, I see?"

"That's right," replied Sergeant Cooper," and I have Ajayi in for suspicion of murder; he missed the last court session."

"Hey, put him somewhere nice, okay," Sergeant Cooper slid the paperwork through the slot and then went back to the elevator.

"You see that door right there?" The officer addressed Ajayi through the thick plexiglass. Pod 300 was painted over top of the door. The heavy garage door slammed shut behind Ajayi as he stepped into Pod 300. The dorm smelled of weed and cigarettes and was packed with faces like his: young, black and angry. Ajayi knew from the way all the dudes were clicked up that he needed to find his set.

"What set you rep Cuz?" asked a tall, skinny, light skinned dude with braids braided to the back, a telltale sign for Crips.

"True blue Cuz, westside."

"Aight, you bunk up with Lil Loc. He gone to court, so you got the cell to yourself. Call me Skinny Cuz, I'm Westside 60." The two dapped up, then Ajayi went to put his things away.

Skinny Cuz was now back in the circle with the other Crips. They were talking amongst themselves, occasionally looking at Ajayi's room. Ajayi knew they were talking about him and that they would check his credentials: things like who his big homie is, and does he hold any rank in the hood.

A Mexican dude went to the cell two doors down from Ajayi. The Mexican dude gave a white guy in the doorway a small clear sandwich bag that had broken pieces in it that resembled ice cubes, just smaller. He also gave the white guy a two-inch long gray pipe that was burnt on one end. There was a wall clock that read 1:25 PM.

"Stand by for chow and Bible study!" The officer in the control booth yelled through the intercom mounted in the wall next to the pod's entrance door. The day space consisted of four thick gorged steel tables with built in stools. The tables also had chess and checker boards imprinted on them. Two rows of thick plastic green bucket style seats were stationed in front of a 42" flat screen, mounted to the cinderblock wall. Each row contained six seats closely spaced to one another. An NFL pre-game show was on. There in an end chair sat a young black guy, light skinned with very thick, eight-inch dreadlocks. He sat quietly watching TV. Ajayi made his way out of his dwelling place for the night, Skinny Loc waved him over.

'Sup, Cuz?' All the Crips welcomed him.

"Line up at the door for Bible study." The security officer followed up.

A short stocky Crip laughed out loud. "Aye, they talking to you church boy."

The young man got up from his chair, walked over and stepped in the middle of the gang bangers.

"What, fool?" The same shorty said, punching the meek young dude.

"I'm sorry." The dude said wiping the blood from the corner of his mouth. "I was going to ask if maybe you wanted to join me at Bible study tonight."

"Do it look like I need Jesus, fool?"

"Hey man, fall back, he tryna do right, aight?" Ajayi said, stepping in front of the young man.

The Crips all eyed one another and felt some type of way. Ajayi walked the young dude back to his seat. "Hey thanks, my name is Ishmael."

"I'm Ajayi. Look man, you might want to stay away from the homie, especially since you ain't bout that life, you feel me?"

Ishmael didn't say a word. He picked up his King James Bible then turned to face Ajayi, "Wanna come? The Lord is always looking for new disciples."

Ajayi immediately thought about Pastor Briggs and Tristan again, and the Tree of Living Water was becoming ever clearer to him. He would reconsider the invitation the pastor offered to him. "Nah, I'm straight right now."

An hour went by and the score between the Dolphins and the Vikings was tied. "Ajayi!" the officer yelled out through the speaker. "Report to visitation."

Ajayi reacted to Skinny Cuz knocking on his cell door. "Aye! The police said you got a visitor, cuz."

There were eight visitation booths at the mezzanine level of the Pod. Ajayi walked up the steps and saw his mom, Alicia, sitting patiently in booth number three. She held the hard black, plastic phone earpiece to her ear, although she was already talking to him through the plexiglass. Ajayi knew that she was just anxious to talk to him.

As Ajayi wiped away the smears from the 3x4 plexiglass, he could see that his mom kept wiping away her tears. "Hey," she said soberly.

"Don't sound like that mama, I'm straight."

"No, you're not." She screamed catching him off guard, also causing the visitation officer to take a casual walk past her booth.

"Somebody's little girl was murdered, Ajayi, and you sit there like it's fine? Baby, God gave all of us a conscience. Please tell me you still have yours." Alicia was crying hard now.

Ajayi lowered his head. After years of banging and seeing death all around, that last comment by his mom hit home. Maybe he should give God a chance. He looked up into his mom's eyes, Alicia reached for her son and she could see the consciousness in his eyes that she'd just questioned him about.

Chapter 16

Psalm 1:16

Pastor Briggs stood examining the '87 Grand National.

"Piece of junk," Mrs. Chum said as she dumped her mop water out of the basement side door.

"I beg to differ. With a little work, this o' girl would make someone a proud owner," the pastor said, stepping closer to where she stood wearing a green and white flower patterned, house dress.

"Junk like I said, who are you anyway, police? You here to arrest that bad boy? Very bad!" she stressed waving her index finger.

Pastor Briggs laughed to himself. "The Bible says we all fall short. Romans 3:23 states, "For all have sinned and come short of the glory of God." Briggs stood there with his hands on his hips proudly.

Mrs. Chum mumbled something under her breath, then stepped back inside and slammed the door.

"Works every time," Pastor Briggs whispered returning to the car. The pastor thought back to the drive by shooting that took place in front of the house of God. He was here at Shannon and Tamika's house to re-extend his offer to Shannon about helping around the church.

The weather was nice, spring was right around the corner, two weeks away. The man of God was used to being around death both spiritually and bodily. He'd seen and touched many dead bodies over the years, but it was the spiritually dead souls that he fished for.

"Pastor," Tamika said walking up the driveway with shopping bags hanging and cutting into her hands. She was dressed in a black body suit with a pink three-quarter length fur coat, shielding her from the late winter wind, blowing occasionally.

"That'll be me. Here, let me grab a couple of those," the pastor casually responded.

"Thank you, my fingers started cramping two blocks ago," said a weary Tamika.

"Tamika, why don't you invest in transportation?" more concerned than curious Pastor Briggs probed.

"Wow!" she said, scraping her feet against the welcome mat at the bottom of the front step. "Home sweet home," she uttered stepping inside the warmth of the front hallway. "C'mon in pastor, please set those right over there." She pointed towards a deep freezer, on the other side of a half wall separating the dining room and front hallway. "And as for a car, no sir! I'll never get behind a wheel. My mother died in a car accident when I was thirteen and on that day, I made a promise to myself to never ever drive if that's the price you pay."

"Tamika, we all have fears, but God helps us overcome them." Pastor Briggs looked into the living room, then down a hallway leading to the back of the house. "Where's Shannon?"

Tamika filled a coffee pot full of water, then placed it on the surface of a hot plate. She wiped her hands with the apron now tied around her waist.

"Well, I don't know what came over him, but he actually attended high school today." She looked at the time on the microwave, "2:20 PM, that knuckle head should be walking in at any minute now. You like your coffee black or light with a touch of sweetener?" She asked.

"Black would be fine. Yeah, I dropped by hoping to check in with him, I want to know how he's been after the shooting and all." Pastor Briggs is now seated at a mini wet bar facing the kitchen.

Tamika removed an apple pie from one of the shopping bags, "You want my honest opinion? I think this generation of young people are becoming accustomed to violence. One of their friends or someone from school gets murdered everyday it seems." She sliced into the pie and placed the wedge onto a small plate. Tamika sat it in front of the pastor along with a fork. "You want ice cream?" She asked smirking. They both looked out the side window. A single ice patch stretched across the backyard and into the alley.

"No thanks, I got enough chills out there. In response to your last comment, you're right. This millennial generation is exposed to early gun accessibility. The internet encourages them, not to mention the gaming wizards, companies and programmers responsible for the introduction of violence in video games," quipped the pastor.

"Wow! That's really good pie, thank you so much!" the paster said as he held a thumbs up.

Tamika stopped pouring the steaming coffee at the sound of the lock unlatching on the front door. Pastor Briggs stood to his feet, wiping the sides of his mouth.

Shannon walked inside and stood to the side, holding the door for Cynthia.

"Excuse me," Tamika said walking into the front hallway.

"I can explain ma, just hear me out." Shannon stood holding his hand out. The young banger was dressed in a black and white patterned denim tunic, with black matching pants and boots. Cynthia looked really nervous. Her two separate ponytails were twisted to where they sat on top of her head, and they had a shiny gleam to them. Her beautiful ebony skin was bright. The red lipstick she wore brought out the soft curve of her jaw line. She removed her sky blue, denim jean jacket, then folded it over both her forearms in front of her stomach. The navy blue, long, Bally dress hung low over her black Bally boots.

"I'm waiting young man, and it better be some good explaining."

The four of them went to the living room. Shannon sat beside Cynthia on the money green Italian sofa. Pastor

Briggs prayed silently as he took a seat in a lazy boy recliner. Tamika remained standing, tapping her right toes on the plush burgundy carpet. Her eyes dashed back and forth from her son to the young lady she'd caught in his bedroom not too long ago. Tamika was also curious as to why the two were holding hands.

Tears began flowing down Cynthia's face. Shannon squeezed Cynthia's hand, "You wanna tell her?" He asked, looking supportively into the young lady's eyes.

Cynthia shook her head "no," then leaned her head on his shoulder, a gesture that said exclaiming the news was also placed on his shoulders to deliver.

"Boy, what's going on?" Tamika asked with concern now.

"We pregnant."

"What? Shannon you're seventeen, baby, with no job. How on earth can you afford a baby?" His mom asked, shocked and concerned, rhetorically not expecting an answer.

"I got this mama."

"You got this? Oh yeah, mister big bad drug dealer. Life is real Shannon! Do you know how hard it was for me raising you?"

"Hey..." Pastor attempts.

"No, please pastor," Tamika said politely to the man of God. "I worked my but off for you, and what is she going to do if you get caught up in those streets? What if some fool...?" Tamika's voice trailed off! She clasped both her hands to her mouth and broke down at the thought of what could be.

Chapter 17

Matthew 5:44

"What's that?" Janelle asked Ajayi pointing at his wrist, as they both sat in Trigonometry class the next day.

"Don't know. Think they call it a dog tag."

"Dog tag? Dog tags are like a necklace that hangs around your neck like in the army, like on a dog's collar.

"Yeah! I don't know. They placed it around my wrist as an arm band identification thing when I was in jail, and when I got released this morning, I just never took it off."

Janelle, shocked, began breathing fast and hard. "You were in jail?! For what Ajayi?" She turned in her desk to face him.

"Hey, it's a long story, and besides it's one I don't care to revisit."

"Excuse me young lady, but do you mind turning to face the front? The exam starts in five minutes." Ms. Lamar, their trigonometry teacher said.

"Yes ma'am." Janelle responded spinning around. "We need to talk!" She said to Ajayi through lip service.

Ajayi nodded okay but thought about his overnight stay in the country last Friday. The events of that night would probably have shaken the average person to the point of being scared straight in a sense. But Ajayi strapped up as soon as he got in his mom's whip, because he was about that life! Banging was a part of his DNA.

Something did click for him that night though. The look in his mom's eyes, a reverent awe, Ajayi could tell she was apprehensive about his safety. The fact that he kept a tool at his side at nearly all the time made him feel that he was safe. But his mom didn't see it that way.

Ms. Lamar's voice snapped Ajayi back into the classroom. He locked in and scored a ninety on his exam. He gathered his things and went on to his mom's. Today was special. His childhood friend, Tristan, would be released from the hospital ward. Ajayi and his mom would give him a ride home.

The sun was bright in the sky. Destiny filled the air as school buses drove in and out of the school's parking lot, bringing students home for the day. Ajayi stood patiently beside the bike rack near staff parking in front to the left of the school building. Birds chirped loudly, a clear sign that spring was in the air. The different array of flowers gave off their scents while dogwood trees lined the grass separating the sidewalk and exterior walls; Snowflakes morphed into snow white dogwood blossoms transforming the landscape with a soft textural beauty that made one thankful to be alive, regardless of their situation. The array of spring colors enhanced the school with a warm rosy welcoming atmosphere.

Ajayi dusted yellow pollen from his pants. "Who you tryna look pretty for?" Janelle asked with her purse dangling on her wrist. She tapped the screen of her smartphone with her left hand. Janelle popped a bubble loudly with her chewing gum as though she impatiently waited for an answer.

"It ain't that kind of party ma, my man is going home today, I'm happy for him ya know."

"For real? Tell him I said what's up with his fine self."

His mom's car horn interrupted the awkward moment.

"Yo, I'ma holla, ma" Ajayi gave her a kiss on the cheek, then hopped in his mom's car.

"Look at you! Boy don't be bringing no grandbabies my way. A sista still livin', I might wanna step out!" They both laughed.

"Hi Ms. Cole" Ajayi spoke to Tristan's mom.

She was in the back seat, "Hey baby, you doing good in school?" She asked in the middle of a coughing spell.

"Girl, I told you to leave them cancer sticks alone." Alicia said turning into traffic.

"I keep asking God to help me."

"It takes faith the size of a mustard seed and the power of Christ for you to not even touch' em girl."

Ajayi sighed loudly. "Ma, don't start with all that preaching please."

Ms. Cole laughed in a way that caused Alicia to stare her down in the rearview mirror.

"Anyway! Let's pray before we get to the hospital. That same demon is coming back to attack Tristan again, at least that's what my Bible says. He needs a lot of encouragement." General Hospital is just like any other major city's sick and injured institution. The emergency room received victims of all kinds of crises: gunshot wounds, stab wounds, burn victims, and assault victims. The hospital had been featured on CNN news as one of the nation's leaders in cancer research where their doctors are coming ever so close to a cure that could save lives.

At the hospital, Tristan waited for them to arrive in the visitor's lobby. Mentally, he hadn't quite gotten over the shooting. Still the overwhelming presence of Christ during his out of body experience by far outweighed the darkness Satan tried to bring into his life. The gang banging lifestyle was still there, some of the homies sent money and cards, but Ajayi was the only one who kept it one hundred by being at his bedside, even more so than Tristan's own family, and that spoke volumes.

Lately, Psalm 22:10 occupied Tristan's mind. The scripture was tattooed on his heart now, and it first came to him in a dream. The Lord quoted it to him, "I was cast upon thee from the womb: thou art my God from my mother's belly." A Psalm from King David, Tristan realized that his current condition was not by coincidence and knew that he was an anointed vessel ordained to spread the true gospel of Jesus Christ. And that was why he joined General Hospital's ministry vowing to comfort others with the love and support God has given him.

"Hey Tristan, they didn't have orange juice, so I got you apple juice instead." Handing him his juice, Tammy, his discharge nurse, said, "That's fine, it all goes to the same place. Remember to take your medicine on time, and refrain from all mood-altering drugs."

"Yeah, yeah, I know. This makes the thousandth time we've gone over this."

"Well it's vital to your health. A couple of inches either way, and you may not have made it. So please, shake your frustrations and follow the instructions."

"Aight, I will."

"For real Tristan, don't just blow me off."

"Real talk, I got you."

Chapter 18

Matthew 6:33

General hospital was situated down by the high line of the industrial section downtown. Built with distinct groups of productive enterprises on the westside, the hospital sat on the corner of High Street and JFK Blvd. Norfolk's barge yard was located directly across four lanes of traffic on the other side of the green handwriting of Olympic Park. The visitor's parking lot was between the Platinum Culture Museum and the hospital itself.

Alicia drove past the blue cabs lining JFK Blvd. She turned into the v-shaped driveway where patients were picked up and dropped off. She rolled her car to a stop under the carport, stopping off to the side just in front of the pedestrian crosswalk. Ms. Cole was the first to exit the vehicle. It was a blessing to have her only son back home. God gave him another chance and one he would use to spread his testimony as far as the eye could see.

Tristan's choices in life vexed his mom's soul up until the day he told her of his decision to share the gospel of Jesus Christ of Nazareth. That's when God granted her a comforting reassurance that Tristan was anointed. Ajayi was the second one out, and the nurse held out a clip board with Tristan's release papers.

Tristan spotted his friend Ajayi and nodded his head, "What up," he said through the hospital lobby window. It had been a couple of months since the incident, and Ajayi was glad to see his friend's color returning to his skin. There was a sheen about the teenager, almost a heavenly glow. Ms. Cole signed the papers then gave them back. She then wheeled her son out the door into a new life.

"Home sweet home," Ajayi said as they pulled into the driveway. Tristan and his mom lived in a dingy yellow stucco two-bedroom apartment with dark green shutters. Black dirt patches replaced the one green lawn the property had. Many of the neighborhood kids would cut through their yard and had worn a foot path straight into the empty lot next door. The path crossed the alley into the parking lot of Speedy's Mall Mart, a corner store that supplied goods until residents could make it to a bigger grocery store. Tristan sat still for a moment while everybody else gathered their things. It was a joyous day, and they would celebrate his return home with a barbecue.

"Yo man, let's get out." Ajayi said with one leg hanging out of his door.

Ms. Cole and Alicia were taking bags inside the house.

Tristan sat staring at his tan, two door Tahoe, "I want to get rid of that."

"Aight. Is that why you're just sitting there?"

Tristan slowly looked at his friend. "I don't want nothing or nobody reminding me of where God has brought me back from. That's part of the pruning process."

Ajayi shook his head, "Ok. We'll dump that joint then bruh," he assured his friend.

Both young men exited the car and made their way up the steps into the house.

"Surprise!" everyone yelled. Tristan was caught off guard by family, friends from school, and some of his ex-homeboys and girls.

He looked at Ajayi then turned and walked back out the door.

"Aye man what's up?" Ajayi hustled to catch up with Tristan walking down the block.

"Look, I know that it was a good gesture with all them showing up, but like I told you, the past is the past. Now, I don't know who invited our old banging homies, but unless they're willing to learn about Christ, bruh…instead of putting them out, I decided to leave. Go back, y'all can enjoy this day, cool out, whatever. Me, this is time for me and God!" Tristan then continued walking alone.

Ajayi understood, because, really, it took a lot of guts to denounce the set. Ajayi knew he had a big decision to make, and he planned to make the first step this Sunday, only two days away.

Chapter 19

Matthew 2:21

"God created man to have fellowship with him. He also gave us free will, because he wants us to voluntarily return the love that he has for us. Love cannot be demanded, but it is commanded. Still, it must be based on a genuine fellowship of spirit, relationship with God, recognition of need, and a desire to follow his commandments." Pastor Briggs read the quote from a seminar workbook to his congregation. It was Sunday morning and the house of God was unusually packed. However, the number of attendees weren't a total surprise to the man of God, for springtime usually brought many out from the confined warmth of their homes.

"Today's lesson is on crying-out. There is a difference you see, in Psalm 5:2, David said 'Hearken unto the voice of my cry, my king, my God: for unto thy will I pray.'" Ajayi sat with Alicia in the back near the entry. If need be, he had a quick escape route and if not, he would shoot his way out with the borrowed tool tucked in his back.

"I'm so proud of you, baby!" his mom said rubbing his knee.

Ajayi knocked her hand away, "I'm not a little one anymore ma," Alicia laughed and refocused on the pastor. Ajayi refocused on the pastor as well but also on his surroundings.

He ducked low in the passenger seat the whole time his mom drove through 13th territory. He had to be a fool to attend church in his enemy's lair. The church's decorative stained-glass windows vibrated, rattling as the bass from a passing car invaded the premises. Ajayi immediately thought about the orange SRT Charger. He knew in his mind that evil was lurking outside the confines of the church. Really though, he felt safe, because of God and the heat he was packing.

The sermon lasted for twenty-five minutes. "Before we end today, I'd again like to extend a festive invite to our visitors; there will be a luncheon, and you're more than welcome to break bread with us." Pastor Briggs then left the pulpit and walked down the aisle towards the front doors. He stopped upon seeing Ajayi.

"Well praise the Lord! He certainly answers prayers. How are you, young man?"

Ajayi cleared his throat and stood to his feet. "Good sir, this is my mom, Alicia."

"Hi, I'm Pastor Briggs, nice to meet you. Please stay for lunch."

"Sure, we'd be honored."

Ajayi looked at his mom. "It was one thing to take a chance coming over here, but it's another thing to hang out!" he thought to himself. Thirty minutes later, Ajayi sat across from the pastor.

"Please pass the potatoes," the pastor instructed.

The two eyed one another, but not in an intense way. Neither knew exactly how to break the ice.

"Yo, your shirt is dope."

"Excuse me?" Pastor Briggs asked with a perplexed look on his face.

"Proper English Ajayi." Alicia said, taking a bite of greens. Then it hit the pastor that Ajayi was talking about his Ralph Lauren Polo shirt. Gray suspenders were strapped over his shoulders connecting to his gray Ralph Lauren pants. Pastor Briggs brushed at his white shirt.

"Thanks! It was a gift from my ex-wife. God rest her soul."

"I'm sorry." Ajayi followed up.

"No, it's fine, you had no idea."

For a moment, the only sound was the scraping of silverware against plates.

"I'm happy you came. If you don't mind me asking, why did you?" the pastor asked.

The real reason flashed across Ajayi's mind faster than a NASCAR driver racing around the track at Daytona 500. "Really, I don't know. Maybe 'cause everybody close to me does it?" he answered vaguely, cutting his eyes at his mom.

"Sounds like some pretty smart company. David says in Psalm that the Lord was his strength and help. Those people in your life have learned to lay aside those false gods, there's only one true God, you know?" Pastor Briggs took a sip of his freshly squeezed lemonade.

Ajayi adjusted his seat a little bit, but not enough to draw attention to the bulge in his lower back. And while looking at the gravy spread over his mashed potatoes, his thought was, "I could never lay down the thing that's been helping me through this gang life," meaning the 9mm Glock in the small of his back.

"The trials we go through in life are only for a season, son."

Ajayi looked up. "What do you mean?"

"You're not the one with a bull's eye on your back every day."

"No, now that's where you're wrong," Ajayi quickly stated.

"For we wrestle not against flesh and blood, but against principalities and power, against the rulers of the darkness of this world, against spiritual wickedness in high places. That's Ephesians 6:12."

"So, what are you saying? These dudes ain't trying to peel my cap?"

"In all honesty, no. However, those guys are allowing evil spirits to control their every step, driving them to commit evil, selfish acts against others. You're in the same situation, and it's not until a person is born again into the Christ Jesus that they are saved from such evil powers. God will open your eyes if you only believe in Him and Him alone. Romans 10:9-10."

Ajayi marinated on the words from the pastor. After they finished eating, everyone returned to the sanctuary to have a word of prayer before leaving. "Before we go, I'd like to thank everyone for entertaining my company on this fine Sunday afternoon. I want you to remember that fear is torment, but God is peace. "For God hath not given us the spirit of fear, but of power and of love, and of sound mind." 2 Timothy 1:7. It's time to get rid of those things that keeps us under the control of evil spirits, and plant your seed in the womb of faith in God."

Ajayi thought about Tristan's comment about leaving those things behind, the pruning, the Tree of Living Water again, and reality was starting to set in. Maybe...just maybe he could trust in God! Maybe there was a life outside of banging.

"So please, allow the living water of God which is His word to water the seeds planted in your hearts today. Please, bow your heads."

Chapter 20

───────◦⌒◦───────

Psalm 28:1

"C'mon Shannon that's enough bruh… you gon' kill' em," Lil Fab said, pulling at his homeboy's arm.

"Nah, this fool came short, and I told him if he did it again, I was gon' put my hands on him! Just keepin' it a real. You know I'm a man of my word."

"Shannon, get off the crack head." They were in a bando and had been serving work all night. The bloody bag eyed smoker jumped to his feet and sprinted out through the empty kitchen and out the back door. Prodigy laughed as he watched through the planks covering the windows for the police.

Lil Fab's phone rang. "Aye man, turn that joint off, it's been ringing all-night." Shannon said, now sitting on a milk crate.

Prodigy licked the end of a cigar. "Yeah, ever since you put in work on Darius, Lil Fab's contacts have been falling at your feet. It's like these fools worship you like God or something."

"I am a god homie." Lil Fab said, waving an AK-47.

"Stop with the game fam, it's about that time again. Them fools came through disrespecting our hood, shooting up o' girl's funeral, and it's time for some get back."

"I'm down for whatever. We need to use another whip though. I had to park the dodge on the other side of town ever since that night," Prodigy said, handing Shannon the cigars. He then mimicked dribbling a basketball followed by an imaginary jump shot.

"Yeah, I feel you. Can't have you shootin' jumpers on the prison yard," Lil Fab said.

"And you, mister baby daddy, we gotta get you back to yo' baby mama."

"You got jokes this morning, huh?" Shannon said slinging an empty coke bottle at his homeboy. It was going on 9 AM by the time Shannon left the other 13th members back in the top house. Secretly, he needed a change. Truly, how could he raise a child with all the turmoil around him? Cynthia was expecting and had for a month now. Would he be there for the birth of their son? Then there was the ever-mounting pressure from his mom. Shannon looked over his shoulder at the sound of dual pipes behind him. It was Channing, 'The work man,' in his 73' Caprice sitting high on twenty-eight-inch rims.

"Sup, one three?"

"Ain't nothing my dude, just left the shop," Shannon said dapping the big homie up.

"Word. So, you got that then?"

Shannon reached into his pocket removing six thousand dollars, wrapped tight in two bank rolls. Channing took the money then reached under his seat to retrieve a quarter of a brick. "Be safe my dude, I seen cops down at the OQ Mart." Channing said, putting the car in gear.

Shannon looked at the ash black Mac-11 in Channing's lap.

"Nah, you the one that needs to be safe, riding like that," he said nodding at the work man's lap.

"Boy, stop! I'ma shoot my way out." The pipes roared to life as the old school dunk peeled out.

Shannon stood there thinking about the insane look in the big homie's eyes. Shoot his way out was basically suicide by cop. Shannon smelled bacon as he stepped through his front door. His mom and Cynthia were facing one another in the kitchen, talking as bacon crackled in the black skillet. On the dining room table were four spots prepared for household members to eat breakfast.

"Y'all set up too many plates, didn't y'all?"

"Take another look son." His mom pointed to the dining room. Shannon walked around each end of the black and gold wood grained table and smiled from ear to ear at the small highchair down on the end where his mom normally sat. "Grandma gon' feed her lil baby." Tamika said hugging Cynthia. Shannon picked up the small baby blue fork, then the spoon. He looked at his mom. Cynthia was crying and resting her head on Tamika's chest.

Chapter 21

Psalm 1:1

Detective Holder squeezed Morrison's hand tightly as they watched the footage from the neighbor's house, capturing the coldblooded murder of Darius Giles. They watched as the shooter exited from a Dodge Charger, then casually walk into a house party. The neighbor's security system was designed on a two-way line meaning it recorded different angles simultaneously. So, the homicide detectives were able to trace the killer's footsteps as he made his way to the back of the house. The footage ended shortly after the shooting.

Detective Holder stood and walked over to the bulletin board. She pointed to Ajayi. "Bring him in on firing a concealed weapon in city limits without a legal permit."

"Hold up genius. There's not a D.A. within fifty miles who would ask a judge to sign a warrant on the grounds of someone shooting a gun at another black kid. Especially since it involves a murder investigation. We need something a little more solid."

"You're such a party pooper, but you're right... hey, I got it. We'll use a little white lie, you know, make Ajayi think we have something." She scratched her head. "O' I need a vacation," Detective Holder said, flopping back into her swivel chair.

"If you're talking leverage, it might work, but I ain't one to use a lie to bring out the truth. How does that scripture go in the Bible? O' yeah...John 8:32 'And ye shall know the truth, and the truth shall make you free.' Morrison said, standing to his feet.

"What? Let me find out you're a Bible scholar," Detective Holder responded.

Morrison laughed, "Anyway, I'm out, Becky's been bugging me about some new restaurant, something about fresh pink salmon, fried tilapia and sushi. I told her she was confused when it comes her taste in food. Want to tag along?" Morrison powered down his laptop.

"Nah. Think I'll go home and get lost in a bubble bath."

"Okay, make sure you don't stay here too late, I hear there's a big storm coming in a couple of hours. Weather's supposed to be pretty bad." Morrison left after giving her the weather update.

Holder stayed and studied the surveillance footage, searching for any kind of lead, and there it was in front of them the whole time, across the street in a neighbor's window, an elderly man. The sun was setting, and some neighborhood kids riding skateboards whizzed by Detective Holder's white Crown Vic; the car was unmarked. So, some of the rebellious teenagers with cigarettes tucked behind their cars and eyed her shiny detective badge as she stepped from her car. There was a sweet aroma in the late evening air, a warm fragrance lingered from the dogwoods lining the block. The house lights gave the two- story white wood sided home a look of authenticity, and the matching white metal roof with its 8/12 pitch boasted durability. Most of the homes on Lonquest Drive were built in the late 1800's, so this street was home to very distinct historic houses. In fact, of was officially a historic district.

Detective Holder looked behind just one house that sat diagonally from where she stood and exactly across the street where the getaway car had parked. She refocused and ascended the concrete steps leading into the screened in porch. The porch floor was made of black polished pine with a wet look high gloss. The only other piece of furniture other than a dark green breach hanging from the ceiling was a small white wicker two foot by two end table. Detective Holder was in motion to knock but stopped upon hearing the lock being unlatched, then the door opened as the face from the camera footage appeared in a three-inch gap.

"What took you so long?" A midsized, balding, white haired man said. Inside the home was a crisp interpretation of a southern style cottage with beige diamond pattern tiles running throughout the entire first floor. The warmth of light- yellow walls and wood ceilings bolstered old money richness to anyone marveling at the inside of the home. Holder followed the man as he dragged his house slippers across the tile into a small den overlooking Lonquest Drive. She knew he was her guy, because he settled into a worn black leather recliner and began peeping out the window.

"Something to drink?" he asked never looking at her.

"No. I had a Frappe on the way over." Detective Holder informed him, as she turned her smart phone over with the back side laying on the coffee table.

"Pardon me..." she thought about who she was talking to, a man who has probably only drank coffee he made himself for years. Detective Holder brushed a strand of her hair from her eyebrow, "I'm sorry, it's a frappucino drink. It's like an iced or chilled type of coffee mixed with cappuccino, if that makes any sense to you."

"My, my, it's not meant to be..." a disapproving chuckle, "Ah, what coffee's come to be, now that's the craziest thing I've ever heard."

Detective Holder massaged her temple. "Mr. Mullin, can we talk about something that you may have seen the night the young man was murdered not too long ago across the street?"

Just the mention of activity at Cuz's house sparked an impulsive reaction from the elderly man.

"Didn't you hear what I said when I opened the door?" he asked the Detective. "There's always traffic over there: parties, drug dealings...dog fights. I believe that they bury the dogs in the backyard."

"Mr. Mullin, I'm not here to listen to speculation. I need facts."

The old man stood to his feet. "You want facts, huh…? Well here, try these." She watched him stroll down to a very old looking brown roll top desk. He lifted the door and removed a case full of DVD's. Mr. Mullin scrolled through them, removing one. He tossed it onto the cushion next to her. "Nail 'em to the wall."

Chapter 22

John 1:4

"**D**EAL WITH ISSUES IN A GODLY MANNER."

The black letters were spaced accordingly in the display case as Ajayi walked past them on his way into the church. Again, risking his life entering the territory of his foe. But lately he'd felt a boldness, a connection, something that's sustaining him and for the first time ever, he read the Bible his grandmother gave him the night before.

Alicia was excited at the fact that he stayed in on a Friday night watching movies with her, after which, she shared old stories with him. Ajayi knew the pastor would be surprised to see him. The sun illuminated the foyer as he opened the door, revealing one-hundred-year-old wood planks, the culprit of squeaks as he walked inside. The open floor plan enabled Ajayi to see all the way down the narrow walkway past the pulpit into the choir stand where on the back wall had a very large mirrored crucifix of Jesus hanging. Quite detailed, there were vivid lashes rendered all over his body, a wooden crown of one-inch thorns lodged into his forehead and temples, portrayed blood surrounding every punctured wound inflicted by large nails, and tears rolling down his cheeks. Ajayi was fixated to this rendition of Jesus being crucified.

"Know this, that our 'old man' is crucified with him, that the body of sin might be destroyed, that henceforth we should not serve sin, for he that is dead is freed from sin." Ajayi turned to face Pastor Briggs who stood with his hands on his sides.

The pastor wore dingy blue jeans that had holes in each knee. He also spotted a gray T-shirt with the slogan "God is the way."

"How do you do that?"

"What's that Ajayi?"

"Just quote the Bible like that?" Ajayi was now sitting in a black pew.

"Well," Pastor Briggs said as he took a seat while singing out loud. "God wants us to build an intimate relationship with him, one way of doing that is to study his word. Being able to retain it in our hearts is the by-product of diligently seeking him."

"Yeah, but my uncle Damon told me that God ain't white, he's black."

"Hold up, let me stop you right there. God doesn't see color. Take into consideration the mirror painted there. The sign over his head says, "King of the Jews." It doesn't say anything about a particular skin color. In fact, the sign was hung in a mocking fashion."

Ajayi shook his head, "Okay," slowly.

Pastor Briggs eyed the young man's clothing, "Are you here to help paint? Or for a fashion show?"

Ajayi scanned his Tom Ford black and brown checkerboard cargo shorts. He brushed at the light brown V-neck T-shirt with his hand. "Nah. Just reppin' that's all."

Briggs laughed, "C'mon, I got some old stuff in the basement."

Ajayi tried on the heavy steel toed work boots. They weren't quite his size, a little too big, but he made them work.

"Here, you'll need this." Pastor Briggs gave the inexperienced young man a paint scraper.

The back of the church looked a lot differently from the first time he'd seen it. It appeared much larger. The back porch was empty, and some of the planks were missing where he'd bent down weeks ago. Ajayi cautiously stepped into the back yard. The protection in his waist gave him some reassurance.

"Okay, give me a hand with this ladder," Pastor Briggs said. Ajayi took hold of the last prong and walked behind the pastor. They stood the ladder on end, then extended it to where three feet of it was just above the eave.

"See that peeling paint there?" Ajayi followed the pastor's finger with his eyes to a spot where the white paint was basically falling off on its own.

"Why's it like that?" he asked.

"No primer. Still got that scraper?" Ajayi removes it from a side pocket of the 3X overalls he was wearing. "When you get up there, take your scraper and do what the name implies, scrape until you don't see any of that paint hanging, then I'll pass you a brush and some sealer."

"No thank you, I ain't going up that shaky thing."

"Seems to me that bullets flying around my head would be much scarier. I dug a few out of my windowsill, you wouldn't know anything about that would you?" Pastor Briggs picked up where he'd left off scraping himself.

Ajayi looked over his shoulder into the alley; it was a beautiful day. Most of the trees were flourishing with new leaves, and the green hue gave the house tops a revitalized look. The neighbors looked friendly, but there was an element of evil lurking, one that wanted to kill the young man. Ajayi caught Pastor Briggs staring up at him, the pastor saw the concerned look in the young man's eyes. He stood to his feet.

"You're protected Ajayi. That gun in your waist is nothing compared to the power of God, why do you think you're still here? How much murder have you experienced and been around? Neither of those bullets had your name on it."

Ajayi stopped halfway up the ladder. "There you go again. Man, you don't know nothing about being black, nothing about riding for the homies, so miss me with all that. I mean, why does God let things happen? My homeboy, Tristan, got popped and he lived, then Darius got popped, he didn't make it. Man, the list goes on," Ajayi said stepping up another few steps.

"This might sound a bit harsh, but God allows those things in our lives to bring us closer to him. So, take heed to the fact that we didn't cross paths accidentally. I was plugged once. I used to ride with a notorious bike gang out west. We terrorized America riding from state to state, shooting up bars and malls. I remember once, we shot up the sheriff's office, because one of our members was arrested after being caught in bed with the jailer's wife." Pastor Briggs laughed to himself.

Ajayi eyed the white man up and down. "You don't look the part."

"Yeah well, that wasn't my true identity." The pastor wiped the lip of a gallon can of primer. "One thing I can say though, I never felt like I fit in. I thank God that those shots I fired never hit anyone. And to be quite honest, I would aim away from people, firing shots in their direction never at them."

"False flagging," Ajayi said while scraping.

"No. that wasn't it. God had a much greater purpose for my life, he wanted me to help encourage life, not take it."

The two worked in silence for the next twenty minutes until Pastor Briggs yelled, "Lunch break, Sister Evans!"

"It ain't marshmallow hot chocolate this time pastor."

"I can see that the liquid is light yellow," he replied laughing, she laughed too.

"It's lemonade! Oh, who' do we have here?" she asked as Ajayi stepped off the last prong of the extension ladder. "Hello young man, you look well mannered."

Ajayi cracked a polite smile and kept his back towards the alley, hiding the bulge in his lower back. He observed the interaction between the two white- people, critiquing their manners, values and principles which were different from what he learned growing up. Could the scriptures of the Bible apply to him? Would his life change if he harkened unto the voice of the Lord? Ms. Evans opened the lid to her wicker style picnic basket. "Here we go, good ol' PBJ's."

Ajayi squinted his eyes. "Yo, ain't there a Micky O's or something around here?" he asked.

"First, 'ain't' isn't a word young man, and peanut butter is a good source of protein for a growing young man such as yourself, so come sit."

"Oh contraire, but ain't is definitely a word and has been for years, even if it gains disapproval by people like you...check your Webster's," Ajayi rebutted, reluctantly taking a seat in the grass beside her.

"Well alright, I'll just have to take you up on that."

Chapter 23

Proverbs 3:5

Detective Holder had her man. This was the break Detective Holder had been praying for. Lil Fab, a.k.a. Fredrick Battle, was fairly easy to identify after running his face through Norfolk's gang database. The intel on her murder suspect is that he lives with a mom who's addicted to heroin. Their residence is a small, two-bedroom apartment off Haron and Lake, in low-income housing. The fifteen-year old banger proudly wears two tear drops inked in red under his right eye. It is said that many in the hood recognize the tear drops as a signature, one that said he had two bodies under his belt. The note goes on to say, Fredrick is short in stature but with a lot of heart. He's considered armed and dangerous.

Detective Morrison peeped over the top of her cubicle which was over eight feet tall.

"Good news Detective!"

She leaned back, "What could be better than this?" Detective Holder challenged him.

"How 'bout a witness?" A very big grin rippled across her face. One hour later, the two homicide detectives walked into 1163 Gabe Plaza. The government building looked like an auditorium from the outside. Just inside the entrance was a thirty-inch piece of iron art shaped into an anchor, donated to the building in honor of the feds holding down the city and ridding the streets of the most widely and unfavorable criminals the city had to offer.

FBI agents whizzed past the city detective's Rover, speeding, even bumping into Morrison. The relationship between the two entities had never been cordial. Most government agents looked down their nose at the locals.

A fifteen-foot wide marble receptionist desk served as a barrier sitting in front, dead in the middle of the two elevator shafts. Every wall except for the entrance which was all glass, floor to ceiling. It was constructed of green and gray marble. There were three security guards behind the desk.

One stared intensely into a PC screen, a female guard was reading a Homes & Gardens magazine, and a heavy set bald black man had his legs kicked up while tossing a blue racket ball up in the air, catching it as it fell back to earth. Holder and Morrison held their badges out so the black guy could see them. They then made a brief call, "Take the elevators to the eighth floor, then take a left at the end of the hallway." The elevator doors sealed shut with a soft whooping sound.

"It would be nice to sit on my nice round backside and whirl a toy in the air, being paid tax-payers' money."

"Yup! It is nice," Morrison said stepping away first.

"Watch it mister," Holder teasingly warned.

They followed the gray carpeting to their destination. The room was packed with eight by ten office cubicles.

"Special Agent Armbrost," a very rough looking, scruffy bearded, middle aged Jamaican said. "You must be Holder and Morrison, please follow me." The FBI Agent led the way walking with a limp.

"A Kingston accent," Detective Holder said.

"Hey, you think maybe he got that last name from brushing people's arms?" her partner asked.

"You're so corny," she said over her shoulder.

Interrogation Room B, Holder told him it was on the corner of the building with three of the four walls made of glass, boasting a view of downtown Norfolk that many would spend big money to have. Sitting alone, in hand and ankle cuffs, was a fat kid with good hair, dressed in a green jumpsuit. A quick glimpse from Detective Holder, and she guessed that he may be Puerto Rican. There was an arrogant air about him despite being in the custody of the FBI. Holder took a seat across from the kid who was dressed down in a green jump suit.

"I am Detective..."

"I know who you are, I ain't got time for games! Those fools tryna give me life! Let's make a deal," Cuz snapped at the Detective.

"I'm all ears."

{}

Chapter 24

Psalm 1:6

Shannon and Cynthia casually walked together after getting off the train at the North Haron train station. "I want you to stop carrying that thing. Your son and I need you, Shannon." She was talking about the 9mm pressing in between them. Before the young banger could answer, a white church van pulled along-side them.

"Hey there brother," Pastor Briggs said shifting the van into park.

"Yo! What's good pastor? This is Cynthia, soon to be the mother of my child, " Shannon said proudly.

Pastor Briggs saw the blush all over the young lady's face and thanked God for her happiness. "Can I offer a ride?"

"Nah, we straight." Shannon answered.

Baby, my feet swellin', they hurt, Shannon."

"Aye, yeah, maybe so." Both teenagers hopped into the van, and Pastor Briggs pulled away, only to be cut off by a maroon Magnum sitting on 24's. Pastor Briggs stopped short of a collision with the car.

"Aye! White man, you better watch where you're driving," said a tall dark-skinned kid with gold tip dreadlocks jumping from his whip. The young man stood behind the van's pathway. Shannon holding a silver .45 with a pearl handgrip eased out of the side of the van against Cynthia's protest. He snuck along the side while using cars to block his approach. Swiftly, he ran up behind the young thug and placed his .45 against the young man's temple.

"What now, nigga?"

Traffic behind the van quickly threw their cars in reverse and sped backwards. The young man clenched his teeth together, and tears flowed, because he feared for his life. He recognized the voice and knew that Shannon could shoot him right in broad daylight.

"Yo, Shannon man, I ain't know them was yo' peeps man."

Shannon looked at the pastor and saw that the man of God had his eyes closed and his lips were moving. Shannon then focused his attention on Cynthia, who was crying. However, it was the reflection of himself in the driver's side window of the Magnum that caused him to lower the weapon. The cold, deadly, lifeless stare in his eyes caused a flashback of his life. Everything, all of the shootouts, dead bodies, homeboys dropping like flies and the very near torturous thought of him getting shot.

"Step off, bruh!" he told the dread wearing thug.

The tires squeaked as the Dodge fled, cutting off motorists in traffic. Pastor Briggs, Shannon and Cynthia rode in silence on their way to dropping them off. Both the pastor and Shannon occasionally made eye contact, but quickly looked away.

"I have to make a drop at the church," Briggs said turning into the alley of Moreland Ave. He then maneuvered the church van back into the narrow yard. "Hey, could you give me a hand?" he asked Shannon looking in the rearview mirror.

"Could I please use your restroom?" Cynthia asked.

"Sure, it's inside and straight through to your right."

Shannon lifted the five-gallon bucket of exterior wall paint and followed the pastor.

"Man, you did all this?" he asked.

Pastor Briggs grunted as he slung his five-gallon pail up onto the scaffolding.

"Well, I had a little help from a young man much like yourself." Briggs wiped his forehead with a blue handkerchief, befitting given he was referring to a Crip.

Shannon felt some type of way behind the white man's comments. "What? The courts order another nigga to beckon to your every call?"

"The Lord doesn't want you to look at it that way."

"How then? Cause I ain't seen none of my prayers answered." Cynthia stood in the doorway listening to the conversation between her child's dad to be and the white pastor. She rubbed her belly and silently prayed that Shannon would listen and leave the gang life before it was too late.

Pastor Briggs walked over and took a seat on a crate. "Well the fact that you're still alive, standing here today tells me the heavenly father loves you. If my memory serves me right, someone tried to take your life recently." So, He has his hedge of protection around you whether you realize it or not."

Shannon shook at the pastor's last comment. A warm sensation filled his veins, heated memories of Anita's body hitting the train station's platform flooded his mind. "The next time someone talks to me about God, I'ma let em' have it," he said, walking into the alley leaving Cynthia clenching her stomach with tears streaming down her face. Shannon jogged away trying to run away from the pain, he needed to escape all the heartbreak, violence and separation he felt with God. "Why?" he yelled through teary eyes.

"That pain is there for a reason," he heard a voice say as clear as day.

Shannon upped his strap and aimed it in every direction, first in front of him, then to the sides, even behind him. No one was there in the middle of the street, he spun continually trying to find the person behind the voice he heard.

"Shannon, I am the Lord, seek my face!" the voice said again.

Shannon ran down Earl St. as fast as he could, trying to escape the voice.

Chapter 25

Proverbs 24:10

A licia jumped out of the bed and sprinted into Ajayi's bedroom. He was there lying in bed asleep. She let out a sigh of relief, then turned to walk out, but he stopped her. "What is it, ma?"

"Nothing baby, just had a bad dream."

"Okay, why did you sprint in here? Was the dream about me?"

She folded her arms, then sat at the end of his bed. "The Lord showed me that a really evil demon is chasing you Ajayi. I saw it in form of a white bull, and even though there was another one that looked like it, still, this particular bull was the same one in my dream a few weeks ago. His name is M-something Diablo. I know that Diablo means the devil and he's after you. Ajayi, that's not all. This bull was aided by another bull, Vennie or something like that. I still see his name on the wall of the stadium, 'VENENO'. It made Diablo stronger and faster, and this time it caught up to you and buried you in a grave that he dug with his front hooves. The first time, a river of water saved you, but not this time. Ajayi, all I'm saying is God is speaking to me about you. And these white bulls, a creepy albino audience and a bullfighter seemed to be on your side, but the Diablo bull drove his sharpened horns through his body and killed you. Baby, I'm really scared for your life. I... I....I want you involved in more positive things like helping the pastor, like you did a couple of weeks ago."

"It was just a dream ma', I'm straight."

"No honey, those same detectives that arrested you have been creeping around our home just about every day, and then when it ain't the police, strange cars ride by a lot. I'm so worried that somebody's gonna shoot you this time."

Ajayi slid down to the end of where his mom sat, rocking back and forth in tears and drenched in sweat. That was a true tell-tale sign that his mom was seriously worried for him. "Look, if it'll make you happy," he said sighing heavily, "Then I'll go and help out more at the church."

She smiled and laid her head on his shoulder. Alicia sniffled slowly, "I'll try and get those tickets for you next week, for the big VCV game against Villanova in a couple of weeks. Okay?"

"Don't worry about it, ma', Tristan got some for the pastor at General Hospital.

"Okay that was nice of him. How's Tristan anyway?"

Ajayi thought about her question, "Good, I guess. Sometimes, I feel like he tryna be all holier than thou."

"Baby don't do that. I'm happy for him. We need more young people like him who ain't scared to trust the Lord's process. Matthew 10:32 'Whosoever, therefore, shall confess me before men, him will I confess also before my father which is in heaven. Hallelujah," Alicia said shaking with joy.

"Man, how do you do that? Just quote scripture like that?"

"Put His words in your heart, baby. Put your all into whatever God has for you. Ask Him to reveal His words to you before you start reading it." She laughed as she stood pulling her house coat closed. Alicia took a step then looked back at her baby boy. "Ajayi I've never told you anything wrong, but, son, whatever you decide to do whether that's serving God or them streets, go hard baby, keeping it one hundred either way, because to get caught slipping is dead, right?" she asked dapping him up.

That Saturday, Ajayi took the train over to the Phillips neighborhood once more. It rained the night before, so, really, he wasn't quite sure about making the trip. The weather lady on Facebook warned of more showers to come, a seventy percent chance of a pour down. Pastor Briggs wasn't picking up, still. Ajayi chose not to allow this small issue to keep him from keeping his word to his mom. As soon as he stepped from the train, Ajayi saw the same white Taurus that had stalked him a couple of months prior. Like a recurrence of the dream his mom had about a white bull chasing him like the devil, Diablo. The car had just turned off Haron and was now riding away from Ajayi up Earl Street. Wet blades of grass stuck to his boots as he cut through a backyard, two doors down from Christ in All. A pit bull named Gucci, black and brown tiger striped, ran up to the fence, sniffing the air as Ajayi walked by. Without warning, the Taurus pulled up and stopped. Before Ajayi could reach for his gun, two Norfolk gang officers jumped from the vehicle. A tall white dude that resembled Dirk from the Dallas Mavericks and a short, bald headed, black dude that wore a bullet proof vest with big white letters reading Vice Tack Unit. They may have been the living water sent by God to save his life in the first nightmarish revelation given to his mom.

"What's your name?" the taller man asked. He seemed to be the aggressor out of the two.

Ajayi felt rather uncomfortable with the officers crowding his space. Not to say he was intimidated, rather, it was the heat tucked in his back. "Ajayi, man that's my name."

"You thirteenth?" the bald man asked, chewing on tobacco.

"You got me twisted homie, I ain't no sucka."

"Oh, so you a rival. What are you doing in Phillips? Out on sum back?"

Ajayi looked at the white dude, and the other officer saw the question in his eyes. "Maybe we should take this no good, piece of crap in." the black officer said taking a hold of Ajayi's arm.

"Hey officers." All three men focused their attention on the church van, idling in the middle of the street.

"How's everything Pastor Briggs?" the taller gang officer asked.

"Oh, just moving however the Lord wants me to! Hey Ajayi, you here to help finish the work on the church?" A Tree of Living Water extends a branch to rescue Ajayi.

"Sure thing, pastor." Ajayi said, snatching his arm from the grip of the Tack Unit officer. "Yo, thanks man," he said to the pastor as he hopped into the van.

"Not a problem, brother." Pastor Briggs eased the van along. Ajayi stared back at the bald officer through his side view mirror. The officer stood alone in the middle of the street. Almost as if he had a personal vendetta against Ajayi. But Ajayi was starting to feel as if God was watching and actually offering this hedge of protection that Pastor Briggs spoke about.

"That's officer Crawford. Lost his only daughter to a gang murder. Her death was his motivation for becoming a Norfolk officer. Pretty decent man, but sometimes can be a vigilante. He blames all gang bangers for his daughter's death. "You're packing, aren't you?" Briggs asked turning onto Haron.

Ajayi didn't answer, rather just looking out of the passenger side window.

"You like living on the edge huh?" the pastor asked speeding down the off ramp onto Hwy 72 into downtown.

"I don't know if I would call it living on the edge, it's more like a way of life. My lifestyle, you feel me?"

"Yeah homeboy, I feel you."

"You kidding right? It's foul how you just slick mocked me," Ajayi said.

"Is that worse than someone tryna peel your cap?" Pastor Briggs asked holding two fingers in the air cocked to the side imitating a gun.

"Yo man, you sound sarcastic and racist, stereotyping a brother, and where you going anyway?"

"I'm not a racist, just telling it like it is." Ten minutes later, they got off the freeway at 38th and Belleville, just south of TIA, Trinity International Airport. The landscape was different in that for three miles, planted for the public to see was hundreds of two feet tall head stones in the shape of white crosses. Service men and women who gave their lives for the country. Pastor Briggs turned into Honorary Cemetery. The sun was now peeping through the clouds. Shining rays from the savior onto the hearts of those mourning for loved ones. The road through the cemetery curved to the right, giving Ajayi a close-up of sharp pots housing shells that used to be home for many souls. The van stopped a short time later, along the grass and asphalt shoulder.

"Okay, we're here," said Pastor Briggs.

"Ain't no painting out here," Ajayi protested.

"I know. Now, follow me." An old white elderly couple passed the two of them on the way out of the graveyard. The elderly man gripped his wife's tender hand in support. She looked very weak and fragile, and the sad look on their faces delivered a lamentation through dried tears.

Chapter 26

John 1:5

The section of the cemetery the two men were now entering was all civilian, and when Ajayi saw the tomb stone with Anita Scolls etched in it, he stopped dead in his tracks. He had tracked two feet away from her grave, and right next to her plot was a freshly dug grave.

"Why we around all these dead people?"

Pastor Briggs waved Ajayi closer. "C'mon, hop in."

"What? Aye man, don't play wit me like that, 'cause, you don't even know me." Ajayi felt some type of way.

"The Lord gave me a revelation about you, Ajayi."

"Yeah well, seems like God's giving out revelations about me like cotton candy, but I don't get any," Ajayi seemed to realize.

Pastor Briggs removed a small dark blue pocket bible and Ajayi's Glock Z3 with an empty magazine from a deep side pocket on his green and black cargo camouflaged shorts. "You made a choice between the word and gang banging. Now, this is your home, go ahead, lay in it." Pastor Briggs motions with the gun urging the young banger now holding the Bible in his left hand and the Glock in his right pointing to the grave then back slightly to the right of Ajayi's left shoulder in a nonthreatening aim.

"Woah! Man, you straight trippin', I really feel like you tryin' me. You pointing my gun at me and telling me to get in a freakin' grave?" Ajayi slowly puts his hands up and starts to back away thinking, "Is this white man serious, and how do I reach for the nine without getting shot with my own gun and this end up really being my new home for eternity?"

"Ajayi, stop, you need to listen and listen closely."

The man of God flips Ajayi's Glock Z3 around pointing at himself and extends it to him. Ajayi stops, drops his hands walks toward him avoiding the grave and finally retrieves his own tool.

Then Pastor Briggs, having bookmarked Romans 6:23, begins reading aloud to a relieved, but annoyed Ajayi. "For the wages of sin is death, but the gift of God is eternal life through Jesus Christ, our Lord." The reason for our little trip here today is because this is where you're headed if you keep chasing death."

"Why here? Why give my gun back now? Why beside Anita's grave as if I had something to do with her death?" Ajayi asked checking the mag and the chamber of his gun to find that both were empty.

"Because I saw you in the passenger side of the Camaro the day of her funeral, but instead of delivering you up to the police, I decided to allow God, in His mercy, to put it on your heart to do the right thing."

"Oh snap, this dude is a witness to me and Cuz's attempted hit on Shannon," Ajayi thought while clutching his head with both hands still with his Glock in his right, spinning around with his back to the preacher.

Concerned that the pastor was now a liability, Ajayi turned and reached around to his lumbar region and quickly pulled out the 9mm pointing it at the man of God's chest and holstering his Glock.

"Old man, give me one good reason not to end you right now!"

"You know that old camera on the church's back porch...."

Ajayi interrupted. "Oh, that's right....so you got something on me...let me guess...you gave the recording to..."

Briggs cut him off, seized control of the exchange and continued, "The camera... the camera.... that camera hasn't worked since I reopened the place. Ajayi, it's not my job to clean you up. That, of course, means I'm not going to turn you in to the police. I'm here to show you that there's a better way. That way is the fountain of living water, Jesus Christ, and you can become the Tree of Living Water and have eternal life with Jesus in the Father's Kingdom. You can live at peace here on earth knowing that God is who you serve. And when you die, you inherit what your brother and Savior, Jesus, inherits as a co-heir to the throne of God. The pastor then turned to another bookmark, Mark 1:17 "And Jesus said unto them, come ye after me, and I will make you to become fishers of men."

"Look, thank you for all your help, but this is who I am, I get down for mine. All y'all beginning to sound alike... you, Tristan, moms, and all about the Tree of Living Water. But my homeboys need me now, they been there for me, so I'm just returning the favor, you feel me? Loyalty, baby. That's all we really got. That's all I ever knew, that's all I need, and that's the way it's gon' be." Ajayi re tucked the 9mm then turned to walk away.

"The Lord loves you son, and all you need is Him to guide your footsteps. C'mon, I'll give you a ride back home."

"Nah, I'm straight. As a matter of fact, stay out my life, white man."

The last words uttered by Ajayi stung the pastor's heart, because he dismissed the law, and was truly trying to help a lost young kid find a way out. Yet, Briggs understood. He knew that Christ learned obedience through suffering, Hebrews 5:8, and this would be the same for those who believe in Christ Jesus as their Savior.

Chapter 27

———⟨∞⟩———

Matthew 7:12

"**B**oy, they straight laced up in this place," Cuz said checking out Pod 200E. One of three in the government building downtown, green carpeting runs throughout the whole floor, there's sixteen one-man cells with 32" flat screens mounted on the walls in each room. Eight rooms on the upper tier, and eight at the ground floor level. During the day, they could battle one another in Madden 17 or NBA2K17 on one of two PS4's.

Cuz lazily dragged his feet toward the microwave where he would cook a summer sausage as a main ingredient for his burrito wraps that he would eat over the weekend. He eyed a very pretty young sister who worked as security on the floor. The two had been flirting back and forth since he arrived three days prior. She already slid him a touch screen phone. In return, Cuz had $1500 wired to her account. Impressed by such a move, she also informed him that she was from upstate New York and that her family was plugged in.

Cuz set the timer and cooked the sausage in the microwave. He felt the phone vibrating in his pocket and knew Kala had texted him. She stood at the door leading into the Pod, licking her lips. His room was in the corner of the first floor, just under the stairwell. Cuz stepped inside and saw that the news was reporting a murder not too far from his house in the hood.

Cuz walked over to the window and stared into the rain pouring outside his room. Betrayal kept popping into his mind. It hadn't ceased since he made a deal with the state for a reduced sentence in his connection with the murder of Anita Scolls. He also gave up Lil' Fab, a rival, thinking he could divert attention or somehow make things right with his set. But still, he knew he had broken the street code, a serious violation. And, normally, there was equal repercussion in doing so.

164

But he felt safe at the moment, because there were only white-collar criminals where he was being held: white guys arrested for hacking bank accounts, black guys for major credit scams, and some being held until their Visa renewal or the border patrol came and got them.

His phone buzzed again; it was Kala texting.

"I'm the only one on the floor tonight, care for company?" Kala texted.

"Come through," Cuz replied.

He quickly cleaned up, brushed his teeth, then waited on her 30 mins.

After lockdown, while he watched the latest music videos, Kala peeped into his doorway. He hand-motioned her to come in. With a sexy look in her eyes, biting her bottom lip, she opened the door, briefly looked back over her shoulder and stepped in with her right hand on her breasts. She closed the door and pushed him to his bunk forcefully so that he sat down. Immediately aroused, he liked that she was in control.

"I can't stay long, papi." She kissed him on his lips. "I'ma need you to lay on your back and close your eyes, I have a little surprise for you, daddy," she said rubbing on his big gut.

Cuz played along and did as he was told, and she saw the bulge in his pants get even bigger, pressing outward. With his arms spread above his shoulder line, she touched it with her hand and then her thigh as he reacted breathing, inhaling heavily. And then, a quick hard thrust and his eyes opened wide. Suddenly gushing with blood, Kala had thrust a long ice pick up through the bottom of his chin.

She kissed his lips again and whispered a message from the Sintane Cartel, "Surprise....loyalty comes before deals, but you knew that."

Dew was on the ground, and several crack heads stood around the basketball court, smoking cigarettes. The housing projects were quiet at six in the morning. The early morning raid was strategically planned for this time, used as an element of surprise by the SWAT team dispatched by Detective Holder. Her team was parked a block down off of Haron and Lake Street. The last SUV from Norfolk's Westside gang unit fell in behind the entourage.

"Okay we move in five minutes," Detective Holder said, then answering her phone. "Holder here."

It was Lieutenant Edwards with the DEA. "You sitting down?" he asked.

"I don't have time for fun and games Edwards, the fact that you're calling me at 6:07 AM doesn't send a good signal to the senses," she said, putting the heavy Kevlar vest on.

"It's your man, Cuz. They found him with an ice pick hanging from his chin about an hour ago. Turns out, a young chick named Kala Young who's been working security for a month, carried out the hit for the Sintane Cartel in return for a pretty penny. She's pretty shaken up, spilling her guts."

Detective Holder sighed loudly into the phone. "Hold her 'til I can get there."

Edward sighed himself. "How long will that be?"

"Don't know, maybe a week." Detective Holder hung up angrily.

"You okay?" Morrison asked leaning out his passenger side window.

"Not exactly, Cuz was murdered last night."

Morrison flopped back into his seat. "Death's chasing everybody."

Holder didn't answer him, she swirled her fingers in the air and shouted, "Let's roll!"

"You better pay me my money now." Big Shirley screamed at the short Mexican dude running out the back door of her and Lil Fab's apartment. She stomped her foot really hard on the concrete floor inside their tiny kitchen. Shirley screamed, because she was in pain.

Lil Fab sprinted down the steps in white and red Indiana basketball shorts. He was bare chested, holding his strap in hand. "Ma' you aigh't?" Shirley scooted away from her son at the sight of the weapon. "Ma', it's okay," Lil Fab said closing the back door and placing the heat on top of the fridge. He could tell she was high out of her mind.

Big Shirley was dressed in nothing but a dingy, stained, sky blue night gown. Her hair was scruffy. There was a clinging on the back porch. Someone had knocked over the small end table his mom used to sunbathe her flowers. Lil Fab helped his shaky mom to her feet, "You gotta get some sleep, ma'."

Just then, the door handle on the back door slowly turned right then returned to its rest position. Fab went and looked out the kitchen window. Crouched, just outside, were men in tactical clothing with vests and wind breakers ready, Norfolk police in stealth mode.

Big Shirley began screaming at the top of her lungs. "It's right there, can you see it baby? Right there," diverting Lil Fab's focus.

Fab, now panning away from the police back inside towards the corner between the fridge and stove, saw nothing!

"What ma'?"

Shirley ran behind her fifteen year old son, pointing over his shoulder to something Lil Fab couldn't see. "The devil, it's the devil," she repeated, wigging out in imminent danger.

The kitchen window exploded, and a small dark green canister bounced off the microwave door, cracking it. The objects landed on the floor, then blew up with a highly intensified flash. Neither Lil Fab nor his mom could see anything, because the intensity of white light blinded them.

The back door flew into the kitchen, kicked off its hinges. "Down! Down! Get on the ground." Lil Fab's head slammed into the kitchen floor as he was tackled from behind. "Fredrick Battle, you're under arrest for the coldblooded murder of Darius Giles."

Chapter 28

Matthew 7:18

A startled Shannon jerked up from his sleep. The same voice he'd heard in the alley was now talking to him in his dream. His phone read 7:15 AM. Today, he and Cynthia had a general check-up appointment, monitoring her pregnancy.

"That pain is there for a reason." Though strange, those words were on point. Growing up without a solid father figure was trying for the young man. Instead of going on father and son trips, Shannon became intimate with the streets, learning from OG's with deep ties to evil, pimps that showed him how to womanize, dealers who showed him how to cook up crack and junkies who showed him that the element of surprise worked best or as they called it, "catching them slipping." All of this, Shannon didn't want his son to experience, and that's why he hadn't been in the streets lately.

Now sitting on the edge of his bed peering into the streets, he answered a call from 'the work man', "Yo, wassup, homie."

"Boy what's good? Ain't seen you around the shop lately," Channing addressed him.

"Yeah, got a lot going on right now."

"Man, stop flexin', you gotta support your peeps, so get on your grind, Lil homie, or wind up like ya boy."

"My boy?" Shannon didn't get the correlation.

"Look at ya, don't even know what's poppin' in the streets. Lil Fab bruh…! SWAT kicked his door in and took him down on Darius' body."

Shannon stood to his feet, then went and peered out his bedroom window. Mrs. Chum was pulling weeds from the cracks in the sidewalk, but other than that, the block was quiet. "Word? That's why that fool ain't hit my line."

"Right, and they tossed Big Shirley in the nut house, fam. Somethin' 'bout her tryna point out somethin' invisible in the corner like a demon to the detectives. All of it sounds crazy to hear. But aye, check this; your boy, Fab, he wouldn't turn state or nothing, right? I got way too much paper in these streets, homie, to get caught up now," Channing emphasized.

Shannon heard a door slam over the phone, then those familiar pipes roaring to life. "O' boy, you know you ain't built like that."

"Yeah, but real talk, you need to tighten up and get back on that paper chase." Channing hung up.

Shannon looked at the shoe box containing the cocaine on the top shelf in his room closet. Right next to the red and white shoe box was his King James Bible, a gift from a youth pastor, years back. There was a tugging in his heart, like the pull of a strong magnet. The word of God was pulling at him. Shannon suppressed the feeling and went to get dressed, then out the door with Cynthia to her appointment.

When they reached The Children's Clinic, they were taken by a toddler racing around a small red and yellow daybed in the waiting area. The little boy had his long curly black hair pulled into a ponytail. His cute little black and white checkerboard Vans patted softly on the carpet as the energetic little man giggled and chased absolutely nothing at all.

"That's gonna be our son." Cynthia said rubbing Shannon's knee.

"I don't think so, my son ain't gon' be crazy like him."

"Shannon! That was so mean!" she chastised him with widened eyes and raised eyebrows.

The two of them laughed to themselves.

"Cynthia Palmer," a midwife nurse called, standing in front of a glossy white pine door. The young prospective parents followed closely behind, eager to learn more about their soon to be first born. The midwife led them into a small room with a desk built into the sheetrock wall. A small stool like roller chair sat in front of it. Across from the desk was a bench style bed with a dark brown cushion spanning the length of the wall. "Please have a seat up there and the doctor will be with you soon," she pointed and advised them.

"Why you look so nervous?" Cynthia asked him.

"Cause we dealing with my lil mans." Shannon's phone vibrated.

"Yo, what it do, Prodigy?"

"Man, riding down on these fools, and I got a dime on some get back. You down?"

"I stay down. Who we talking 'bout?"

"Aigh't then. Them fools that rode down on o' girl funeral."

"Let's get it." Shannon hung up. The look on his face was one of concern. He watched as Cynthia laid there while the same nurse took her vital signs. Her heartrate, blood pressure, and temperature were all normal.

Cynthia took hold of his hand, "What's the matter?"

Shannon shook his head, "Everything is fine baby momma."

She smiled, "Okay, baby daddy."

Later that night, Shannon thought about the smile on Cynthia's face the whole time they were with the midwife.

"Aye man, you good?" Gomez asked serving the junkie from the hole in the wall.

Shannon snapped out of his thoughts.

"Don't watch me! Keep your eyes on that money!"

Gomez had taken Lil Fab's spot in the trap house until he returned or someone else with a hustler's mentality could take over. Gomez was eager but for the wrong reasons; he liked to stunt, flash his money, and spend it at topless bars. Gomez didn't possess a Bally's swagger.

The trap house door opened, and Prodigy walked in wearing Gucci down to his socks. In his hand was a matching duffle bag. "What it do, fam?" he asked Shannon.

"Swimming in the dough baby," Shannon, call 'em 'rubber-band' man', flashed serious bankroll.

"Aye, we moving on them fools soon. Check this out." Prodigy unzipped the bag. Then removed two flat, black FNS 9C's. He gave Shannon one, "Think you can handle that?" he asked his homeboy.

Chapter 29

Matthew 8:2

Tristan crossed JFK, and out through the breezeway of the cultural museum. For weeks now, this had been his routine every day at noon. God had touched his body, healing him completely. He didn't even take the aftercare meds provided to him. God also placed it on his heart as witness to his homeboys, reminding Tristan that it was time he let the light of the savior shine in their lives, but like most who rejected the savior, they pushed him away too. Jesus told the disciples to shake the dust off their feet and move on, an act that indicated that they were washing their hands of unbelievers and taking their message of the gospel elsewhere.

In the crosswalk of 3rd Ave., Tristan ran into Duane Morrels, a military veteran who paraded outside General Hospital showcasing a 4" long white cross on his shoulder. Duane was sold out for Jesus and tried to spread the gospel of Christ to everyone who walked through the doors of the hospital. On this day, Duane had the cross laying across his right shoulder and an American flag over his left.

"Tristan, my brother in Christ, you here to spread that word, huh?" Duane smiled, revealing a full gold grill.

The twenty-six-year old veteran walked with a limp; he left the military with an honorable discharge and a medal after being injured by a roadside bomb in Iraq. In Duane's testimony, he shares how an angel nursed his wounds until help arrived. The angel also told Duane that he was now a vessel for Jesus.

"You know it bro. What's with the flag?"

Duane looked at the red, white and blue flag, colors that are meant to unite the nation although not so with arch-rivals, "Supporting my country, brother. Hey, got something for you. My nephew gave me a couple of tickets to their rival game against Georgetown. I been saving them for you."

"Wow, thanks man, I'm a big fan of VCV!"

"Oh, God is faithful, by whom ye were called unto the fellowship of his son, Jesus Christ our Lord. 1 Corinthians 1:9. How are things coming with your old homeboys?" he asked.

Tristan sighed wearisomely.

"I'm truly fishing for men in vain. It's like throwing a baited line out there, but the fish aren't biting."

"Yeah well, in season brother, trust me, they hear you. Hey, sorry to be rude dude, but I gotta go, meeting a friend for coffee." Duane said hugging Tristan.

"Okay, love ya bruh, be safe." The glass doors parted as Tristan walked in range of automatic sensors. Just a month prior, he had been wheeled out of those same doors.

The hospital waiting lounge was packed with family, friends, and other loved one's there in support of hurting loved ones going through trying times in their lives. Prospective patients sat in check-in booths, some clutching themselves in areas of pain and others with faces of concern as they did their best to describe the issues they were dealing with.

Tristan examined the college basketball tickets as he rode the elevator to the third floor. A ding sounded as the elevator stopped at his desired floor. Balloons, action figures, flowers, and candy wheeled by as Sandy, the floor's clown, made her rounds.

"Hey Tristan, how's everything?" Nurse Phaedra asked sitting behind a desk in the nurse's station.

"I'm blessed and highly favored." Tristan signed in and walked toward room 316A just down on the left of the west wing. The door was open, welcoming anyone needing a hug as they were freely given inside. Tristan easily stepped in.

"You don't have to tippy toe around Tris." Bianca coughed softly after addressing her big brother; at least that's how she saw him. The two developed their relationship after her surgery during which she lost a lung due to cancer. Bianca now was awaiting a lung replacement in hopes of a match soon. She was one of Tristan's first recruits for Christ.

"Didn't know if you were sleeping or not," Tristan said standing over her.

Bianca looked pale, because her pigmentation suffered as a result of side effects from her constant radiation therapy. A feeding tube was attached to her side, slowly pumping a liquid diet into her. Bianca could barely move, requiring assistance with everything. He patted her right hand, careful not to disturb the inserted I.V. needle.

"Hey, let's pray in," both of them closed their eyes, and Tristan began to pray. 'Praying in' simply meant going to the throne of God, seeking his wisdom for a fitting topic of conversation that the two would have. "In the name of Jesus, Amen." Tristan ended.

"Okay, fill me in on your week," Bianca requested. She liked to hear about things that happened around the city.

"Well, I went to see Tyler Perry's Boo."

"What's that?" she coughed again.

"You need some water?"

"Yes, a little, please." Bianca sucked slowly through the straw as Tristan held a cup with apple juice. "Thank you."

"You're welcome." Tristan said.

"Now about the movie."

"Yes, the movie. Well, in the movie, Madea wards off killers, creepy poltergeists, ghosts…"

"Hold up. Did you say ghosts?"

"That's right." Both Tristan's and Bianca's eyes fell upon her mom, Ava, as she walked in carrying a single pink balloon that read "Jesus loves you."

"Hey guys." Ava said in a likely manner. Ava was a single parent because Bianca's dad, Kanye, skipped out on them.

"Hey ma, uhm...I don't think we can fit another balloon in here."

"I know honey, it's the thought that counts, right... Tristan, the cat got your tongue?"

"No, Mrs. Daniels, how are you?" He gave her a warm hug.

"Whew, it's been a rough week, but we know all things work together for the good of those who truly love Him and who are called for his purpose! Right?"

"Amen," he responded. "Excuse me, but can you finish with Madea?" Bianca anxiously prodded.

"Oh yeah! There's zombies, haunted houses…"

"Hey, wait a minute, I don't mean to be disrespectful, but we ain't 'bout to invite no evil spirits up in here."

"What do you mean?" Bianca asked sitting up slightly.

"1 Thessalonians 5:22 says "Abstain from all appearances of evil." Meaning it's not okay to talk about or watch such things." Tristan felt instantly hot from an adrenaline rush. By no means did he want to invite such a thing into the presence of God.

"I'm sorry, Mrs. Daniels, I wasn't aware of that scripture."

"It's okay honey, these people snatching Bibles out of schools so fast that the children coming up won't have a chance to know of such a scripture either. So, you ain't the only one baby, but the Bible is very clear about entertaining the right spirit, and that's the spirit of the living God."

"Here, let's read some more of these words of life." Tristan and Ava stood around Bianca's bed as Mrs. Daniels read from the King James Bible.

Tristan studied the way Ava respected, recited and cradled God's holy word. He also noticed how Bianca's countenance changed as the word of life saturated her heart.

Chapter 30

Psalm 11:3

"And David danced before the Lord with all his might; 2 Samuel 6:14" Pastor Briggs shouted into the microphone. Just what kind of dance or walk does your family, friends, or co-worker see? What kind of person are you? Dancing before the Lord? The Bible says David did it with all his might. I'm here to tell you, friends, that there's no in-between, either you're with God or you're not! We also know from the Bible that there's no middle ground, straddling the fence or lukewarm spirit acceptable to God. God will only turn away from such behavior, character or lack of commitment." The congregation watched as Briggs walked from behind the pulpit dressed in a gold and purple robe. The man of God walked down the two steps over to the table prepared for communion.

"I want to invite all in this intimate fellowship. However, I must also warn those who need to get their hearts right with the Father before we partake of this communion. Please take a few moments to clear your hearts."

Sister Evans gave Pastor Briggs his King James Bible. "I'd like for you to turn in your Bibles to Mark 14: starting at verse twenty-two. When you get there, say Amen." Pastor Briggs cleared his throat, then Deacon Hanson and Deacon Stevens picked up the wine and bread to distribute to the congregation. "This is the Eucharist, the time of the Passover in which Jesus ate for the last time with his apostles just before he was crucified." The Christ in All sanctuary was silent. The whole church was locked in on the words of life.

The church said, "Amen."

Pastor Briggs, already at Mark 14:22, began to read;

"[22]And as they did eat, Jesus took bread, and blessed, and brake it, and gave to them, and said, "Take, eat; this is my body." [23]And He took the cup, and when he had given thanks, He gave it to them, and they all drank of it. [24]And He said unto them, "This is my blood of the new testament, which is shed for many. [25]Verily, I say unto you, I will drink no more of the fruit of the vine until that day that I drink it new in the kingdom of God.""

Pastor Briggs led his congregation in communion, then the church let out.

Later that night, Pastor Briggs drove in silence, thinking about Ajayi and their encounter weeks ago. "My choice of words could have been better." Briggs thought as he turned into the parking lot at Norfolk County Jail. Inside, Smitty greeted him, and they followed the same routine as usual. "Praise the Lord," Briggs shouted. The man responded the same way. Halfway into the service, one of the inmates stood to his feet. A tall young man, brown skinned, low temp fade with a single tear drop on the left side of his face said, "Aye sir, God told me to tell you that the young man you been dealing with...whatever his name is, you need to warn him tonight, sir! Let him know that death is chasing him. A single demon will try to kill him real soon."

Pastor Briggs said, "God was referring to Ajayi."

"Tell ahh...tell Ajayi the storm is coming, but Jesus is with him. Also, in these storms, it's hard to find peace but in Jesus is that peace exists." The young man went on to say.

185

"For He is our peace, who hath broken down the middle wall of separation between us; Ephesians 2:14."

Pastor Briggs could only praise God.

Chapter 31

Zechariah 7:9

Georgetown's senior guard, Dominic Young, crossed VCV's guard, Jamil Johnson, by putting him on skates. Then slam dunked the game winning ball with .07 seconds left on the home team's clock. The gymnasium fell silent after its "Defense" chants fell defenseless. Ajayi and Tristan watched as Duane's nephew Kwahi stood in line shaking the winning team's hand.

"Boy, that was a nail-biter!" said an excited Tristan.

"Straight up, o' boy was ballin'!" exclaimed Ajayi boiling with adrenaline and joy.

The Crowns began clearing the gym as quickly as they could.

Shannon and Prodigy sat masked by the tinted windows of Prodigy's stolen navy-blue Chrysler 300.

"O' girl gave me the dime on this fool after meeting him at the train station. One thing about females, they can break down the strongest playas to nothin', for real."

"True dat," Shannon responded to his homeboy.

The time was just after 10:15 PM, and this was the university's only night game of the year. The students exited the building in single file. Samantha, a younger white female, loved the hood life, and many shot callers used her to lure rivals and customers into their traps. The blank check headed beauty had met Ajayi while waiting to go home after spending time in the Philips hood with 13th street members. She told them about meeting Ajayi, and word got back to Prodigy, who wanted to holla at Shannon. She and Ajayi spent a lot of time communicating via internet. Shannon held the FNS 9C in his hand waiting for the right opportunity.

"Aye, bruh… y'all get 'em next time," Tristan encouraged Kwahi. "Man, it's all good, we still headed to the tournament." Ajayi tagged along, texting back and forth with

Samantha. He thought it was strange how she was able to pinpoint their exact location knowing their movements.

It had been thirty minutes since the game ended, so the parking lot was nearly empty as they walked towards Kwahi's Tahoe. Shannon and Prodigy pulled the ski masks down over their faces. The light flashed, and the security system sounded as Kwahi unlocked the SUV. Shannon crept along the tall green hedges on the edge of the sidewalk in between the gym and parking lot. Prodigy followed close behind. Both crouched low, just fifteen feet from the white Tahoe. They could hear the three men laughing.

Shannon yelled, "13th," then started bussin'.

Ajayi dropped his phone at the sound of 13th as the back window of the passenger side exploded, sending projectiles of glass shards like missiles straight at Ajayi. Several found their target and at least one hit the bull's-eye... Ajayi's right eye. Twelve to thirteen more shots fired, and then it became silent.

No, man, stay down bruh! Your eye is bleeding bad. You alright, though? We gotta get you to a hospital!" Kwahi said. Squealing tires painted the asphalt with liquid rubber from the burnout as the Chrysler ripped the tires spinning away.

"Nah man, I'm good, where's Tristan? An eerie silence arose as Ajayi sat up with ringing in his ears from the gunshots. Just behind the SUV, laying in the grass, was Tristan.

"Tristan, Tristan!" shouted Ajayi.

Tristan was silent.

Ajayi strained with his left eye, trying to tell whether his friend was okay since he wasn't responding. Ajayi and Kwahi moved closer to Tristan. What they saw was robbed them of their breath. His VCV game jersey was gruesomely bloodied, peppered with at least four bullets. His body lay lifeless. The realization was quite surreal, and it seemed that everything switched to slo-mo cinematography. The extreme shock of his friend's lifeless body lying there, caused by the ghastly horror, turned the lights out on Ajayi; he fell unconscious. Kwahi, shocked and confused, refusing to believe what had happened, fell to his knees in hyper slow frames, seemingly in a stupor.

Alicia rubbed her son's arm gently as he had been sedated with anesthetics. She couldn't believe how she almost lost him the night prior. The death of Tristan put the community in a state of uproar and mourning.

"How is he?" referring to Ajayi.

"The doctor said he'll be fine, but one of the glass shards scratched his pupil, and he's got several other cuts and scratches from the impact of the shards," Pastor Briggs said. Alicia began crying again.

"I'm so tired of worrying, I'm so tired of this gang banging mess."

Pastor Briggs gave her a hug.

"I don't know what to do anymore, I'm thinking of sending Ajayi to Atlanta with his auntie on his daddy's side of the family. We talk a lot on Facebook. Catherine always wants to know about him."

"Have you prayed for guidance in this situation?"

"I've prayed, fasted, followed him to school, I'm so exhausted."

"What is he doing here?" Ajayi asked about the pastor.

"I called him, and he's been praying for you non-stop, so show some respect." Alicia snapped between sniffles. She then walked out of the room. Ajayi turned his head toward the window, looking outside. The dreariness of rain falling outside only added to the misery.

"When are you going to stop putting yourself and your mother through all the torment, physical pain, and emotional distress?" uttered the pastor.

"I see you still walking around with that judgmental holier than thou attitude," Ajayi said.

Pastor Briggs walked over and blocked Ajayi's vision. The young banger tried to sit up, but the aching in his head was unbearable. He felt at the gauze over his eye.

"Why? Why did God take him? Tristan changed men, he comforted people. He wasn't throwing up a set anymore, he wasn't even packing, man. I had the gun, but I didn't have a chance to save him. I couldn't save him, I... I... I couldn't!!" Ajayi said, breaking down and bursting into a loud, head throbbing, heart-felt cry.

Pastor Briggs stepped closer, but *God told him to stop. "That pain is there for a reason," The Lord dropped into the pastor's spirit.*

Chapter 32

2 Samuel 22:2

A week later, the church was packed with many who knew and loved Tristan. His mom, many ex-gang members, and choir members paid their respects, love and sorrow was there next to Tristan's coffin pouring out many tears. His mom refused to leave his side as he lay there.

Pastor Briggs preached about forgiveness, a word that caused Ajayi to sit with his head down, lost and void, repelling the words of the service. All he wanted was revenge, because the hate and pain were trapped too deep within the cavern of his heart to extract it with a helicopter rescue team and a gurney even. During the week leading up to Tristan's funeral, Ajayi collected guns and rallied the troops amid his mom's protest.

"The second greatest commandment is to love your neighbor as you love thyself. Sometimes this is hard when things happen out of our control, or when we live a lifestyle outside of what God has in store for us," preached Briggs as he stepped down from the pulpit and walked directly to within six or so feet of Ajayi. "Let God repay your enemy. Let God direct your steps."

Ajayi snapped his head up, rising as anger rose within him. The crowded church let out a loud gasp as the hurt banger jumped to his feet with a strap in his hand. Tears streamed down Ajayi's face as he slowly walked to Tristan's coffin.

"Aye bruh… I was listening when you said you didn't want anything reminding you of where God has brought you back from." Ajayi forced out a laugh to dilute the pain.

"I want to learn about God man, but he makes it so hard when things like this happen. Look at you bruh… he could have taken one of them.... Aaaahhh!" Ajayi yelled at the top of his lungs. Alicia stood to her feet, leaving her heart in her seat, taking a step towards her son, but Pastor Briggs held her back, quickly grabbing her hand.

"I'ma make this right though. That's on the hood bruh... R.I.P. homie." The congregation, including his mom, watched Ajayi tuck the handgun into the small of his back, then walk down the center isle and out of the church.

Chapter 33

Psalm 31:4

Detective Morrison skidded to a stop outside the basketball court at People's Park, a well-known park where college, mini-level and NBA players hooped. The area is readily noticeable with a striking 94" regulation sized basketball court. Black and green, surrounded by bleachers and concession stands, as well as vendors who sell everything from fake apparel to hair weave imported from China. Thirty- foot tall spruce trees hovered over each end of the court, providing shade for fans and both team benches.

Detective Holder pushed her way through the crowd. Tupac's "I get Around" pumped through speakers mounted on streetlamp posts. The parking lot was packed with fans and bystanders. Security was out in force guarding high profile vehicles, including those in the NBA section where people took pictures beside a custom, orange Bentley Flying Spur belonging to legendary baller, Allen Iverson. They also guarded a VIP section, houses nearby, and NBA scouts, critiquing potential draft picks.

The two detectives stopped at the edge of the court. "Well, there goes identifying him by height. They're all like trees, we just need to figure out where his roots are planted," Morrison yelled over the noisy crowd.

"I think I see him." Holder said. "There, with the Florida Jersey on."

They watched as the young man went up with two hands catching an alley-oop. "He's pretty good," Morrison yelled.

"Let's go!" Holder yelled back.

The detectives, followed by four officers, walked right into the middle of the game. Referees blew their whistles while running towards the intruders. "Hey! What are you guys doing?!" the head referee asked.

Detective Holder stopped him in his tracks with her badge. "Your pal, Fredrick, suggested we pay you a little visit," Morrison told Prodigy, placing the hand cuffs on him.

"What? Who? Aye, my parents are lawyers," Prodigy protested.

"Good! You're gonna need 'em, because you're under arrest in connection with the murder of Darius Giles.

Shannon gave Cynthia a kiss and rubbed on her small bulge; at the two- month mark, she was starting to show. With his mom at work, they took the time to chill and enjoy one another's company. Up until the last shooting, Shannon stayed gone, and his absence was starting to affect her. Shannon jumped to his feet upon seeing Lil Fab's and Prodigy's mug shots flash on the six o' clock news. "What's wrong, ba...?" Cynthia began to ask, but stopped short, noticing Shannon's two friends on the news. She turned the volume up and slowly walked around to stand in front of him. "Authorities have arrested these two in connection with the murder of Darius Giles and are looking for a third suspect."

"Shannon baby, please tell me you're not that third person! Please baby!" Cynthia clutched her stomach.

"Look, everything's gonna be aigh't." Shannon caressed her face.

"People are dying, don't that mean anything? God gave you a conscience, your son! No, our son. So, he's supposed to walk these same streets?! When is it gonna stop?" she asked.

A horn honked and Shannon looked out the screen door. It was Channing. "Aye, I'll be right back." He started to leave, but she stopped him. "

"I want to go to church Sunday."

Shannon smirked then tried to leave again. "No Shannon, I want to go to church Sunday. I'm so proud of you baby. You haven't been hanging out in them dangerous streets around those no-good homeboys of yours. Plus, I'm glad you decided not to bring that gun with you this morning. You're starting to realize and respect God's house."

Truly, Shannon was coming around to trusting Jesus as his savior. God was revealing Himself to the seventeen-year old gang banger. His mom, Tamika, was noticing the sudden change in her son.

"Aigh't, Sunday, we'll go to church."

Word on the street was that Prodigy decided to take the hit on both murders, allowing Shannon a chance to be a dad. This, they both agreed to over a phone call.

Sunday Cynthia nor her baby daddy paid any attention to the Monte Carlo as they walked past it. Many other churchgoers filed in anticipating a helpful word from God. The two soon to be parents fell in line with the rest of the sheep.

Ajayi slapped the clip into the bottom of his Glock and opened the door. He watched the last person, an older black woman dressed in a baby blue dress suit wearing a white hat with a white and yellow bow tied in the front. Ajayi scanned up and down Earl St. then shut the door behind him. The weapon in his hand felt heavy, because scripture rained down from memory, flooding his mind: 1 John 3:15

"Whosoever hateth his brother...is a murderer, and ye know that no murderer hath eternal life abiding in him."

Chapter 34

For two weeks now, Ajayi has been searching for Shannon, and today, he finally had the dime on his enemy, thanks to some good intel from Samantha. She told Ajayi she wanted to help and that she wanted revenge on Shannon, "After seeing him all lovey-dovey with his baby mama," in her words. "That nigga shouldn't have played me."

On this Sunday morning, the sun was shining brightly, unusually bright. It was as if the sun's rays were aimed directly at the money green Monte Carlo Ajayi sat in on Earl St. two doors down from Christ in All. Samantha told Ajayi that for the past two Sundays at 11 AM, Shannon and his girl showed up for services at Christ in All. Ajayi was there to avenge Tristan's murder, a promise to the homie he would fulfill. Hate, anger, and pain all played the driving forces that lead Ajayi to this point in his life.

While suppressing the tugging at is soul, God was providing a way out of this. "This is it for me. I'm getting out after this," he thought, pulling the ski mask over his face. Shannon and Cynthia casually walked up Earl Street towards Christ in All Church.

A voice played in Ajayi's head, "You are about to commit yet another murder; and ye know that no murderer hath eternal life abiding in him." Ajayi heard the choir as he ascended the concrete steps. The door handle felt warm to his touch. As he stepped through, just ahead stood the fifteen-member choir, along with the praise and worship leader. Pastor Briggs sat on the right, nodding to the music.

Reality slowed to a virtual standstill, slo-mo cinematography, just like the night Tristan was capped as every step seemed to weigh Ajayi down. Cynthia sat hugged up under Shannon's armpit as he sat next to the isle in the new pew. Ajayi spotted them then raised the tool, aiming at his rival walking within a foot of the young man. The congregation screamed at the sight of the weapon, causing

Shannon to look over his shoulder right into the barrel, then into the blackened eyes of Ajayi.

Pastor Briggs shouted "No!" and jumped from his seat.

Cynthia waved her hands at Ajayi screaming, "No!"

And then, there was a pop!

The End....*to be continued.*

Appendix

Disrespecting the House of God, dishonoring his grace, reveals the most heinous evil. Surrender to Jesus and live.

"Glory be to God for inspiring me to write this book, I honor and love you Lord."

Edited by Angelica Polis and Lori McCaskill